GREEK WAYS

**Other books by Phil Andros
from Alyson Publications**

Below the Belt & Other Stories

The Boys in Blue

Different Strokes

My Brother, My Self

Roman Conquests

Shuttlecock

GREEK WAYS

PHIL ANDROS

ALYSON PUBLICATIONS

LOS ANGELES

Manufactured in the United States of America.
Printed on acid-free paper.

This trade paperback is published by Alyson Publications Inc.,
P.O. Box 4371, Los Angeles, California 90078.
Distribution in the United Kingdom by Turnaround Publisher Services Ltd.,
27 Horsell Road, London N5 1XL, England.

First published by Grey Fox Press: 1975
First Alyson edition: February 1992
Second edition: October 1996

5 4 3 2 1

ISBN 1-55583-396-9
(Previously published with ISBN 1-55583-223-7
by Perineum Press, an Alyson Publications imprint,
and with ISBN 0-912516-84-4 by Grey Fox Press)

Contents

GREEK WAYS

1. By the Seashore

I guess you've really never lived until you've lain on your back on the sand, head on your folded leather jacket, and looked out at the broad blue reaches of the Pacific through the hairy legs of a young surfer.

He was facing out toward the Pacific, too, and was very busy. He squeezed a coupla inches of grease out of a tube, and reached around backside with his right hand, while with his left he pulled one cheek of his ass wide. With a practiced aim he laid the grease right on the small brown puckerhole, the gate of heaven, and then he tossed the tube onto the sand, and looked around smiling over his shoulder, his long blond hair blowing a little in the ocean breeze.

"Ready, man?" He had a strong deep voice.

I got two fingers around the base of my cock and pointed it straight up. "Yup," I said.

I was perfectly flat, my legs spread. He spread his even farther, and—still standing—planted a foot on each side of me below the kneecaps. Then he stiffened his arms, held them behind him at an angle, and fell backward.

It damned near scared me to death. I flinched, but he didn't see it. He must have had some training in gymnastics to do a thing like that. It was odd to see him in such a four-point position—his weight resting entirely on his two feet and his two straightened arms. The muscles of his back and shoulders were ridged and hard.

Four points? It was really five. He let his body sink slowly downward, while I—helpful to the end . . . *his* end—guided ole Betsy straight and true towards the small inverted U formed where the cheeks of his ass came together—a kind of curve I'd rarely seen, and visible only when one was stretched out like an upside-down daddy-longlegs, as he was.

The grease was still cool, not yet warmed by his body heat or the sun, and I felt my cockhead touch gently, sink in and then stop, because his asshole was not yet open. He rested easily in that tensed position, finally beginning a series of small up-and-down movements, very gentle, pushing my cock—now stiff as steel and sensitive to the tiny folds and ridges of his asshole—harder each time against the closed ring. I felt it give a little, and then reached up with my hands to his hipbones (the skin silky-satin-soft), and using some pressure held him steadily balanced on my cock. The head was already halfway in, and now it was my turn to start a few movements of my hips, prodding easily and gently at the folds of the asshole—still, still defeated by that damned sphincter! Then I felt it give a bit more, and suddenly I was into him, into that red-warm cavern so often explored, yet so continually new . . .

He sighed faintly, and the tension in his arms and legs relaxed. He lowered his body down on mine and, with a gentle circular movement of his ass, he ground lightly against my pelvic bone. I reached up around his flat belly—beginning to be moist with the sun and the sweat of his exertions—and pulled him close against me, crossing my arms over his chest, my fingers finding first one nipple and then the other, which I rolled between thumb and forefinger. He was not unpleasantly heavy upon me.

I raised my knees and dug my heels into the damp sand to get more leverage, and then started to fuck him, long slow

2

thrusts which raised his body at its centerpoint, and let it fall again. And he was not inactive. He set up a pattern of squirming, half-circular, half up-and-down, that directed my cock into all the pleasure spots of his ass and probably buzzed his joyspot with every third thrust, judging from the soft moans of pleasure that escaped him.

His nipples had hardened and my hands left them, sliding down his sleek flat belly past his navel to reach his cock. I crossed my thumbs at the base of it and fitted my hands down alongside his heavy balls, my fingers pressing hard against the little bridge between his cock and asshole. His cock was rigid and upstanding. I could feel it but I could not see it, with his head in the way. And I was a little distracted, too, I must admit. That long blond hair fell right in my face, so that I was unconsciously turning to avoid it or else trying to get it out of my eyes and mouth without making too much of a fuss.

"Hey!" I said suddenly, after this nineteenth-century dalliance had gone on for about five minutes.

He turned his head a little. "Yes . . . what?" he asked dreamily.

"Man, you may be havin' the time of your life," I said, my hand giving his cock a few up-and-downs for good measure, "but it's hard for me to come this way."

He said softly, "How you wanta do it?"

"Get up on your knees," I said. "I'm gonna fuck you doggy-doggy."

"Whatever turns you on," he said. He began to lift his upper body and I lifted mine along with his so that we didn't break the connecting rod.

He crouched on his haunches and I put both hands into the tight-pressed curve of his belly and thighs and lifted him up a trifle, so that the angle was better.

A lot of things go into the making of a good fuck. In this position I could see the Pacific, and watch the waves breaking against the striated grey-black shale of the sandy cove.

And I could also look straight down and see the thick length of ole Betsy — shining in the sunlight with the grease he'd put on — driving in and out, in and out, turning the lips of his ass first inward, then outward, and, by God, I was feelin' burly and dominant, and sea-shouldering. I felt the sun all along my back and legs, warm and sensual, and the dampness of the packed sand on my knees and shinbones. I could raise my eyes from my cock and see the long, slow needles of turquoise and pearl breaking in the air as the waves hit the tortured rocks. It was no distraction from the fucking, but an added enjoyment. And I could look lower to see the long, lean muscles of my surfer's back, hard-bunched and tanned to a deep sienna, with tones of copper and rose. His tightened, small ass, even in this position, did not have the pear shape of a female's; the lines of it were straight and good, and its muscles worked diligently under the smooth brown skin, as he reached for my cock with his ass, clutching it on the in-thrust and then tightening the canal as I drew outward.

He was enjoying it, and I was too. He kept up a soft moaning, with small whinnies of pleasure now and then as I passed a really sensitive spot.

"Oh, fuck me!" he said softly, and clutched me hard.

Sometimes you pick up your own enjoyment and pleasure from that of others. I could have screwed him for an hour, it felt so good, but when he said "Fuck me!" it triggered my own response. I felt the tiny hairs of the nerve endings all over my body suddenly flame with the approach of the orgasm, and then from the nape of my neck, rapidly descending the stairway of my backbone, came the first flash. It concentrated in my groin and balls, swirled through the hidden secret tubes and vesicles, zipped back up to the pleasure center in my brain.

And then, just before the first shot came, I had an impulse. I drew my cock out of his ass, and gasping, straining, toes bent under, with my cock laid straight and hard up the crack of his ass, came all over him, my gyzym springing out of me

4

without control, thick white gouts of it landing halfway up his back, and still pumping, pumping, laying itself in long lines of white over his muscular ass, and sliding down one asscheek to lose itself in my pubic hair and down around my balls.

The orgasm was so intense that I fell down on top of him, smearing my gyzym all over his back and ass, and my belly and balls. My weight pressed him farther down, so that he was almost in a fetal position in the sand. I rubbed my chin against his backbone, still gasping.

"Whoo, man!" I said. "A real nature-fuck."

He turned around, managing to get the hair out of his eyes, and smiled. "Like Whitman," he said.

". . . and Emerson and Thoreau and all the rest," I said, exhaling deeply and lying contentedly against him.

"Why'dja take it out just before you came?" he asked.

"Just an idea," I said. "I wanted to see it spread all over you."

He wiggled his ass a little, grinning. "Well, you sure as hell got what you wanted. I feel like you've broken a jar of library paste between us."

I laughed. "No sweat," I said. I reached farther back and got a handful of warm, dry sand. Then I wiped his ass and back with it. The gyzym came off like magic. "See?" I said. "An old Boy Scout trick."

"That's a troop I'd have my doubts about," he grinned at me. He scrambled up from his haunches. "Here . . . lemme do it for you." He grabbed some of the sand and went to work on me, rubbing it all through my pubic hair, down between my thighs, and gently over my balls. Then he took the tips of his fingers and tried to flick the sand out of the hair around my cock while he held on to the shaft. He couldn't get all of it. Finally he got down on hands and knees and blew into my pubic hair. I laughed.

He looked up, grinning. "Don't you say it," he said.

"I won't," I said. "It's too old and too obvious." Then I

looked at him. "Well, what'll we do for seconds? You oughta have your jollies just like me."

"I was hopin' you'd say something like that," he said mischievously. "How's about swappin' cans?"

I groaned, pretending I didn't like it. He had a gentlemanly-sized prick, about six and a half inches against my nine, but it was fairly thick. Then I said, "Oh well, I suppose I could take it. After all you oughta have your full twenty bucks' worth."

"I been dyin' to get into that Greek ass of yours," he said, twinkling. "The cradle of civilization."

"You're not the first," I said.

He looked at me. "You've got a good hard body," he said. "Good definition. And man, that hair pattern really turns me on. Just right . . . a lot on the chest and down around your cock, and just enough to connect the two. How old are you anyway?"

"Twenty-nine," I said. "And you?"

He shrugged. "Twenty-four next month."

"How do you like hustling?"

"Oh, I guess it's all right. I like the money, and I sorta like some of the older guys, even if they're not beauties. They're kinder . . . more considerate."

"More grateful, if we can believe Ben Franklin," I said. I picked up the tube of grease and squeezed some out, and then laid it at the back door. "Okay, sexy . . . howja wanta do it?"

He looked at the ocean. "Let's get some of this damned sand off us first," he said. "That is, unless you'd enjoy a sandpaper fuck."

"The water's too damned cold," I grumbled. "Besides, it'll shrink you all up until you ain't got no cock."

He laughed. "We won't stay that long." He held out his hand. "C'mon."

"Okay," I said, but was damned if I'd take his hand like a schoolgirl.

I grabbed a cake of soap and we ran toward the curling

ocean. Curiously, San Gregorio beach — about thirty miles south of San Francisco, past Half Moon Bay — was about the only area the fuzz hadn't been able to control when it came to bare-ass beaches. The main section was for the straights, but we club members had a little cove all to ourselves at the northern end. Time and again the cops had tried to bust us, but to no avail. For one thing, the approach was difficult, and there were volunteer sentries, so that should the centurions arrive, everybody was draped.

At nine o'clock on a May morning, San Gregorio was absolutely deserted. People were working or going to school or doing the thousand things that the poor wageslaves had to do to get enough money to buy enough food to make enough energy to get up and go to work to get enough money to buy enough food . . . shit! it was a tiresome cycle.

Davey beat me to the water, but I was underneath first. The shock of it was strong — cold and biting, and yet foamy and caressing. I stood up and was promptly knocked over by a breaker I hadn't seen arriving, while Dave was dancing about and hollering some ten feet away. I looked myself over and saw the sand was gone.

"C'mon!" I yelled. "That's enough." Then I remembered the soap in my hand and, standing thigh-deep in water, tugged this way and that by the waves, I lathered my pubic bush and washed my cock in the Pacific. It was astonishing how clean San Gregorio beach was, considering the pollution at all the others. Tides, I reckon.

Davey was already back at the spot where we'd been screwing, toweling his blond shoulder-length hair and looking like a woodland faun instead of a merman risen from the blue. I ran up to him and grabbed my own towel. Drying my short curly black hair was less of a chore than his was; I gave a coupla swipes at my back and thighs and drew the towel between my legs and up my front, shivering some from the Pacific breeze.

"As I was sayin', sexy," I said. "Howja wanta do it?"

Dave grinned. "I wanta watch the Pacific too," he said. "So how about you gettin' on your back with your legs up?"

"Hell," I grumbled. "Then I can't see the ocean myself."

He laughed. "You'd think we were here just to watch the waves," he said, "instead of fuck."

". . . and you're bound to get me down in a woman's position," I said, although it didn't really matter to me.

"Well, isn't that what you are?" he said, but he grinned.

I flicked the towel at him and caught him square on his tight-packed handsome ass. "You bastard," I growled.

"Ow," he said, pronouncing it instead of yelping. He was a good-looking dude, all right—about six feet tall, like me, with real yellow hair to which the sun had added a lot of white-gold. His eyes were pale blue and his face rather narrow, but with a strong chin and deep-carved lips, the kind that you could just imagine fitting over the head of a cock. He had the long lean muscles of a swimmer's body, a broad chest, and blond hair on his legs, with a sprinkling of it gathered in the center of his pectorals. His nipples oddly enough had deep-brown areolas, and the nipples themselves stuck out like little round-end cylinders.

"Damn," I said, looking down at ole Betsy. It had shrunk back into the confinement of the black hair of my crotch. "My cock done got washed away."

Dave laughed. "I wouldn't want to fuck a man without a cock," he said. "Lemme see if we can't find it."

He dropped his towel and got on his knees in front of me. The full-carved red lips I had imagined around my cock now were nuzzling in my crotch; they found the head of my cock and closed over it, warm and exciting. I interlocked my fingers at the back of his head and felt ole Betsy begin to expand, lengthening and thickening, growing longer by slight, small movements until my cockhead touched the ring at the back of his throat and slipped slowly through. I moved my hips a little forward.

His air was cut off and it couldn't last long. With a gasp he opened his mouth and withdrew my cock. "Whew!" he said. "Didn't take long to find it again."

I tousled his hair with one hand. "Okay, asshole buddy," I said. "Let's get goin' before the world arrives." I looked down at his cock. It was up and ready, and the muscle holding it tight against his belly had not yet been broken by years of wearing tight elastic briefs. The flaming cocktip just touched his navel.

I reached back to my ass and gingerly poked a finger there. Neither the sea water nor the frontal scrubbing had disturbed the grease; it was still in place. "So you want me on my back," I said.

"Yup . . . please," he said.

I lay down on the sand, picking a warmer spot, raised my knees and spread them wide. "Okay," I said, "let's see what you can do."

He put some additional grease on his cock, stroking it lovingly, and thumbing the head and frenum. Then he got on his knees between my legs, reached down and caught them, and hoisted them over his shoulders. He was amazingly strong. I locked my ankles behind his neck.

He was hard and ready. I reached down to guide him in but he pushed my hand away. "I'd rather do it myself, mother," he murmured, and we both laughed.

The kid knew how to fuck, for sure. There was no sudden lunge, no feeling of I-gotta-show-what-a-man-I-am to this fuck. It was slow, with easy pushes against the locked ring, little ticklings around the outer edge of my asshole, small squirmings, and yet you sensed the strength of his hard-muscled thighs and strong ass as they forced his cock slowly forward. His long hair fell down against my chest and its movements against my skin were like a drift of butterflies across and against my nipples.

I was a sudden-opener type. The ring gave way as if someone had turned a key, and he slid in, groaning with pleasure. I didn't feel too bad myself. His cock, once in, seemed larger and more satisfying than it had when I looked at it. My asshole was distended pleasurably, and in that position—as he slowly moved straight in—he hit my joyspot head-on. I moved my head back, neck muscles straining, and moaned involuntarily.

"Hurt you, man?" he asked softly.

"Anything . . . but," I gasped. "You . . . hit it . . . just right."

He started to screw me. There was nothing fancy about it—no side movements, no poking around, just a wonderful straight in-and-out fuck. He must have sensed that was the thing which gave me the greatest pleasure, and what's a fuck anyway? Yeah, you want to get your own rocks off, but you want to bring as much delight as possible to your partner.

Only once before in my life had I felt anything like it. Each stroke brought me ecstasy, each thrust made me feel the way I imagine a cunt feels when she's getting a really good screw. He seemed to know how to time his strokes just right, so that he kept me in a continuing state of head-moving from side to side, happy little moans escaping from me, my ass and pelvis thrusting forward to meet each push that brought me such delight, the pleasure spots in my brain stimulated again and again until I felt the pearls seeping out the end of my cock. Dimly I remembered how much I had felt like a woman on that spotted, faintly malodorous bed in Paris, with that superbly expert Armenian making me almost come with each inward thrust. My prostate was evidently so placed that only in that leg-up position could it be prodded and caressed. Meanwhile young Daveyboy was speeding up, and I could feel his body tensing. He was not far away from coming. With that, despite the unutterable joy I felt, I began to thrust forward more, to clamp the muscles of my ass tighter, and suddenly, his heart against mine, I felt the arrival. And just as I had done, he withdrew. A gout of his gyzym hit me on the chin, and others, eight or nine, caught me on the belly, ran into my pubic hair and slipped down around my balls—a real storm of semen, white and thick.

"Decided . . . to do . . . the same thing, huh?" I panted.

Gasping, he nodded, his fair hair against my neck. "Just . . . wanted to see . . . if I could . . . put out as much . . . as you," he said.

"More, I think," I said. "Sheez, what a mess!"

He moved his head. "There's all . . . the water in the Pacific . . . again."

I unlocked my ankles, and looked at myself. "Hey, buddy," I said. "You really done slopped me up." I took hold of his long yellow hair. "Now I tell you what. You pull your god-damned cock outta my cunt, and I got sumpin' for you to do before we freeze our balls off in the Pacific again."

He raised his head and looked at me. "Wh . . . What?"

"You left all those little Daveys down on my belly and around my balls. And you don't wanta lose 'em, do you? So . . ." I said, pulling his head up and putting my other hand behind it, pushing, "just get down there and clean me off. Lick it all up and swallow it, and lemme hear it go down," I said, pretending a viciousness I didn't feel at all.

"O . . . Okay," he said. He drew back slightly, and then kneeling, began to lick all the gyzym he'd spilled.

That was a grand feeling—his tongue flat on my belly, then edgewise down between my balls and thighs, all over my balls, and sucking what he could get out of my pubic hair. Finally he finished.

"Now come up here," I growled, still holding him by his hair.

And then I surprised the hell out of him, I think, by drawing his handsome face down to mine, and kissing him full on the lips, sending my own tongue into his mouth to lick the inside and around the edges of his lips, tasting the faint monosodium glutamate flavor of his semen . . .

"Cut!" the director bawled from his position of ten feet away. "Damn, we sure got some good scenes today!"

2. Toes and Things

On the way back to San Francisco, with two hundred bucks for my part in the day's work, I felt pretty good. Jerry, the producer-cameraman-director-and-scriptwriter (what there was of it), sat in the front seat with the second cameraman named Milt, while Jerry's *mignon* drove. I wouldn't say that Jerry was exactly a chicken hawk, but he came close; all his "lovers" were around seventeen. Jerry was about thirty, an easygoing but intense personality, the kind that always wants everything done yesterday — mod-styled brown hair, and handsome enough in a kind of middle-class way, with thin lips and a pleasant personality. He liked to call himself the "foremost smut-peddler of northern California" and he was. His *mignon*, Teddy, had the bounciness of youth, sometimes enough to make you sick, but he was learning the wild and wicked ways of being the sultan's favorite. He'd run away from his home in Concord as soon as he'd discovered he was a club member, about three years ago.. His long shaggy hair really did him good, because his forehead was overly high. Davey, my beach partner, had gone back to the house in his own car.

In the back seat was the third cameraman, a dude named Jim, and beside him sat the star of Jerry's latest blue movie —

myself. In the far corner were the assorted cameras, tripods, and paraphernalia of movie-making.

Jim yawned. Aside from myself, he was the only one with short hair, and his was really short—not only a crewcut but a flattop.

"Damn," he said. "This business of gettin' up at six ain't for me."

The yawn caught me too. "You're right, buddy," I said. "Think you got some good shots today?"

He smiled. "Hell, man, I was right in there, two feet away, for at least half of it," he said. "Of course they're good. What I can't understand is why you never noticed us at all."

"Concentration, m'boy," I said. "When you're fuckin', you don't want to be distracted. Least of all by a camera."

"If this film's a success I 'spose your hustlin' rates will go up," he said.

"Double," I said.

"I'd kinda like to have you before they do," he said.

"Speak to the arranger," I said, nodding toward Jerry. "I'm in his stable now."

"I will," Jim said.

I had never really paid much attention to Jim before. Now I looked at him. He was about twenty-five, good strong shoulders, black hair, and a generous mouth. His eyebrows were black clear across; evidently he had the same problem I did with their growing together. He had on a pair of old Levi's that he'd evidently been wearing ever since he left Indiana, and he also had a hardon.

"I could hardly keep my eyes on the camera," he said, "while you were fuckin' Dave. I kept imaginin' myself in his place."

"Why not?" I murmured. "There's always time for one more."

". . . and your feet," he went on. "Damn, they're beautiful. You oughta go barefooted more instead of keeping them in those engineer boots."

I grinned, and then happened to notice a small lavender button high on the lapel of his windbreaker. "What's your button say?"

He put his thumb under it and aimed it closer to my eyes. I read: "Toes Are For Sucking."

"Sheez!" I said. "That turn you on?"

"You've no idea," he said.

"Why?"

He shrugged. "Symbol of maleness, I 'spose," he said. Then he looked at me. "You've got the most beautiful feet in the world. I couldn't keep the camera off 'em."

I laughed. "Jerry'll fire you for that," I said. "He's a cock man himself."

Again that shrug. "Couldn't care less," he said. "Y'know . . ." and he turned halfway to face me on the back seat, "sometimes you have to go through hell . . . even blow guys . . . just to get at their feet."

"Not me," I said. "I like it."

He lighted up like a switchboard. "You mean I can have 'em?"

"Sure. For free."

He looked at the three in the front seat, busy talking. "Right now?" he asked.

"Why not?"

I bent over a little, undid the buckle on my boot and pulled it off, sock inside. Then I too turned halfway in the back seat and put my leg up over the camera equipment. There was more than ecstasy in Jim's face; he looked as if he had just been promoted from the cherubim to the highest order of the seraphim. He took my slightly damp foot, brushed aside the few remaining grains of sand, laid the sole of it against his cheek, and then bent low in the seat.

"What the hell is going on back there?" Jerry demanded, turning so that he could see.

I waggled my hand at him. "Nothing that anyone could find a law against in the penal code of California," I said.

"I'd like to have that done to me once," said bouncy Ted, so engrossed in watching the proceedings in the rearview mirror that Jerry spoke sharply to him. "Watch your drivin', kid," and then to us, "Just be discreet."

Meanwhile, Jim was busy. He went to work on my Achilles' tendon first, and from there slipped around to the sole of my foot with a flattened tongue. After that he pointed it a little and went exploring between my toes, down to the juncture. I put one hand on his unmussable hair. "Don't you think someone will see us?"

He raised up a moment. "All the cars are low-slung," he said. "And besides, I'm not breakin' any law."

". . . Yet," I added.

He cupped my heel in his hand and raised it to his mouth, sitting well back in his corner, and looked at it. "Classic, man," he said.

Even the little fumbling he'd already done had begun to make me hard again. "Damn," I said, "it's all yours. Get after it."

He started in on the toes, the big one first. Unless you've ever had a guy give you a toejob, you don't know what I went through. My whole body started to quiver almost at once. He sucked my big toe, nibbled at it, took it clear into his mouth, giving it little gentle bites. Then he finished with that, leaving me with a damp crotch and damp armpits and head thrown back. The next point was the cleft between the big toe and the second one, with him widening his tongue so that it laved both at once—giving me a delightful chill. And then he turned his attention to the long second toe, sucking it forcibly, and at the same time flicking his tongue all along the sides and the head of it. So, with the third, fourth, and fifth— pure heaven. I had a raging hardon.

He had a big enough mouth, and I whispered, "Can't you get 'em all in at once?" and he did. I curved my toes downward over his lower teeth, and was rewarded by having his talented tongue slip back and forth over them, pausing at the crevices which were closely bound together by his mouth pressure. His eyes were tight shut and he was handling my foot as if it were made of pearls and rubies.

That one foot lasted all the way from Montara to Pacifica. Then he opened his eyes, leaned across the camera equipment, and said, "How about the other?"

No sweat. He was a genius at it, and reminded me of lil ole Karl in his shoeshop, who was no more talented than this cat was. I quickly took off the other boot and sock and laid my other foot up on his lap. He bent over it like a Hindu at worship in his temple.

"Another one!" he murmured, and started in the same way. Jerry's little-boy darling, Teddy, was fascinated with the procedure.

"Do it to me sometime, will you?" he asked Jim.

Jim, already at work on my big toe, looked up and took my toe out of his mouth. "Anytime, junior," he said.

Jerry swatted him playfully. "Over my dead body," he said.

"You never do things like that for me," Teddy pouted.

"I will, I will," Jerry said.

"I want Jim to do it," Teddy said. "He's an expert. You can be chaperon."

"You damn betcha I will," Jerry said. If he had been a dog, he would have bared his teeth.

From Pacifica into the heart of the city where Jerry had his stable, the traffic grew heavier, and Jim—evidently noticing this—slipped quietly down to the floor of the back seat. I shifted my position and lay back in the corner, eyes closed, and let him take over completely.

"Goddamn it," Teddy, who had been watching in the rear-view mirror, said, "now I can't see."

Jerry spoke somewhat sharply to him. "You can have all the toejobs you want, but right now you pay attention to your driving, huh?"

Junior subsided, I kept my eyes closed, and Jim kept working on my foot. It was like a long ride into heaven. At times his tongue was hard, at times soft, but each lick was a caress, each small stab a delight. The skin all over my body kept reacting, raising itself in small chill-specks of pleasure, and then settling down as Jim moved to another part of my foot. I thought that several times I was actually close to an orgasm, and knew for a certainty that ole Betsy had put out a dozen pearls of pleasure. I looked down once through half-slitted eyes at my chinos, and saw a wet spot there. The sensation was so intense that I was not even aware of entering San Francisco, nor of the ups and downs of the streets. It was only when Junior stopped the car that I opened my eyes and saw that we were at the old house on Mason Street.

"Damn, Jimmy, that was good," I said, drawing on my wool socks and boots. The knights-at-arms had vanished along with the castle of Camelot and the pleasure-dome of Kubla Khan. Even the shower room of the San Francisco Police Academy, with dozens of naked feet attached to young stalwart bodies soaping themselves, offering their cocks rampant—all the fantasies had faded in front of the white door on Mason, with its discreetly drawn curtains. It looked like an ordinary middle-class front, and the passersby could hardly guess what went on inside, nor dream that every day, on the steepest of hills, they puffed past the biggest male whorehouse in San Francisco.

But a sophisticate, one wise in the ways of the homosexual subculture, could tell the minute he stepped inside—not only from the odors of sex and fragrance of lubricants, the lingering smell of tobacco and socks, but from the row of framed photographs of the members of Jerry's current stable, handsome studs (or at least photographed by Jerry's wizardry to appear handsome) lining the corridor wall, offering their pricks front-on or sidewise, lying on their backs occasionally, legs hanging down over the side of the bed. The men willing to be screwed were always posed so that their assholes were at least partly visible. But I had never let Jerry hang my picture among those of the other whores.

It was what they used to call a railroad apartment — a long corridor leading through it to the back, with rooms opening off on each side. And in each room, a number on the door, and a bed, and not much else inside. They were workrooms, no more, for the "in-calls," when we didn't have to go out to a hotel or house.

I made for mine, number seven, and undressed, feeling a bit gritty and gummy from the morning's session. As the senior stud, I had first call on the bathroom, so I threw a towel over my shoulder and padded on naked feet down to the bathroom.

At room number eight, the door was open. Jerry lounged against the doorjamb, arms folded, looking inside. He turned his head and grinned. "Seems like a toejob affects you even after the ball you had on the beach this morning," he said, looking down at my crotch.

I looked down, too, at ole Betsy, heavy and full with the blood that had not yet receded from Jim's accomplished ministrations. "Always," I said, grinning. "What's goin' on inside?"

Jerry shrugged. "You know Teddy," he said. "Once he gets an idea in his head, he can't wait. He had his pants off before we were hardly inside." He pointed with one shoulder.

Teddy, naked except for his flaming red skimpy briefs — which were dangerously tent-poled with his hardon — was lying on the bed with one forearm flung across his eyes, while Jim, still fully clothed, was sitting next to him on the low couch, bent over Teddy's foot.

"I'm gonna see that nothing else goes on," Jerry said softly.

"Madame Chaperone," I said wryly, giving it the French pronunciation.

Jerry grinned. "At least . . . chaperon," he said. "I'll see you later about the 'Madame' part."

From Teddy there came an almost continuous pleasure

moan. The squirming of his body told me of his enjoyment, and I didn't know whether Jerry was waiting there to finish him off or if Teddy would pop without it. At any rate, the situation seemed well in hand.

Funny thing about living in a male bordello, you took such things in your stride. I suppose we were all voyeurs, and yet voyeurs with a kind of cool calculated reaction; we didn't get excited and plunge into the rooms for an orgy. It was all pretty well under control. We stopped, looked, or listened, and if a door was closed on a john and his "model" . . . well, it was closed. Most of the time we didn't even bother to listen to see if the hustler were getting fucked or sucked. Grunts, groans, cries of pleasure had all become commonplace. You heard them without surprise; they were as ordinary as reading the morning paper or eating breakfast. I'd been there about two months, but even from the beginning I did not react to them. Some of the less experienced hustlers got all excited when they looked or listened, but not me.

I punched Jerry on the shoulder and said, "Well, Teddy's gonna want a new treatment from you after Jim gets through with him," and went down the hall to the shower.

There was a full-length mirror on the back of the bathroom door. I closed it, threw the towel aside, and took a good hard look at myself, not too displeased with what I saw, for twenty-nine, the deep end of the twenties when the mold and rot begin. Six feet tall, black curly hair on my head, fairly short, and a big fan of hair on my chest that narrowed to a wrist-wide line as it crawled down the center of a flat belly and below the navel expanded into a tangled thick crisp black bush. And from the middle of that hung a long prick, still swollen and heavy, turgid from the morning on the beach and the toejob, and what I had seen in room eight. I flexed my leg, drawing one knee up, and saw the hard-bunched thigh muscles jump out satisfactorily. The definition was still good—shoulders, washboard belly (from all that subconscious holding-in I'd trained my stomach muscles to do), muscular biceps, hairy forearms and enough on the legs. I was what they call a white Greek, as far as my skin went, but even a little sun turned it dark tan, thanks to my Aegean ancestors from Cyprus.

Ecco Narcissus! I turned sidewise. My butt was large and solid enough, for after all, you can't drive a spike with a tackhammer. It was hollow with a strong deep muscle that, according to folklore, meant you were an active lover. And there hanging out in front, arced satisfyingly downward, was the plum-colored head of the father of all evil, firm enough and heavy, still remembering room eight. I put a friendly hand on my cock and squeezed it, even moving my hand back and forth a coupla times, wondering just how many apertures it had been inside in fourteen years of hustling. And then I gave it a small friendly pat, for after all, Ole Betsy was my bread-and-butter, and I was extremely fond of her.

Enough of this autoerotic dalliance, I decided, and threw the shower curtain back to climb in. It stuck a little at the bottom; a thousand showers had started a black discolortion at the edge where it clung against the tub. With the money Jerry was pulling in from both his movies and his stable, you'd think he could at least afford a coupla bucks for a new shower curtain every six weeks.

The shower left me feeling fine. I dried myself, still watching each movement in the full-length mirror and still saw nothing out of place—no sagging rolls at the waistline, no flab. If I had ever run into someone who looked like me, I think I might have tumbled for him, at least for a night. And thinking that, I remembered my wild chase over our Great Commonwealth, looking for my identical twin brother Denny Andrews, and the inevitable meeting with him (or was it?) there on China Beach under the Golden Gate bridge, the curious feeling on seeing your doppelgänger, and the realization of his cock (or my own?) in my mouth. That little

20

episode had never been really understood or explained, for when I awoke from a doze he was gone (no footprints in the sand), with only a handsome young San Francisco centurion telling me to put my clothes on . . . and blow him. The whole experience remained in my mind as the most mysterious and inexplicable thing that had ever happened to me, the closest brush I had ever had against the dark wings of the unknown and implausible.

There was a timid threefold knock on the door. I frowned. One of the house rules was that when anyone was in the john with the door closed, he was not to be bothered. Nonetheless, I opened it, still frowning.

It was my crewcut toejob man Jim, looking a little upset. I could see his cock poking against the thin fabric of his slacks.

"Yeah, whatdyuh want?" I was none too friendly. He looked down at my feet, then up my body, pausing at my cock.

"Can I come in?"

"Yeah," I growled, throwing the towel across my back and grabbing each end to dry myself.

He came in and closed the door behind him. "I . . . I hardly know how to say this," he said, "but I'd like to blow you."

That's our old whorehouse, all right. Come right out with it, no use being delicate.

I was a bit annoyed at being taken away from the admiration of myself. "I thought you said that it was like goin' through hell, blowin' someone just so you could get at his feet . . . And besides, you're one of the cameramen. Didn't you see enough down at San Gregorio?"

Jim turned pink. "Th . . . that's the trouble," he said. "I saw too much. It ain't very often I wanta blow anyone after I've had his feet . . . but . . . you're different."

I wouldn't help him along. "How different?"

"Ah," he said, some of his courage returning, his embarrassment evaporating. "You got something most guys don't have."

21

"I'm flattered," I said sardonically, and went on drying my legs, first one and then the other. Freed from the water, the hair rose on them, surrounding them with a glinting of black. "Just what have I got?"

"You're . . . sexy," he stammered.

"Oh . . . so?" Despite myself I grinned, and then put one hand on my cock. "You got thirty-five bucks or so for Jerry?"

He swallowed hard. "You know I ain't," he said. "Besides, Jerry said it would be all right. He'd give you your regular cut of twenty if you'd let me."

"Damn generous of him." The truth was that despite my being a little pooped from the morning's action on the beach, his toejob had got me all bothered again. And besides, there weren't any calls for the evening . . . yet.

I leaned my butt against the rim of the washbowl and folded my arms across my chest. I was standing directly in line with the mirror, but then I decided if I wanted to watch him at his labors of Aphrodite, I'd prefer a side view. I took one step away from the washbowl, turned sidewise, and took a stance with my legs apart.

"Okay, toesucker," I growled. "Take your shirt and pants off and get to work."

That was all he had on except sneakers, and he was naked before you could say antidisestablishmentarianism, meanwhile glowing like a sparkler on the Fourth of July.

"You mean I really can?"

"Get to work," I said. "You'd better be goddamned good, because the ole vesicles ain't quite full yet."

He was on his knees in front of me, his hands gripping the backside of my thighs, even before I'd finished speaking. He opened those wide full red lips and took Betsy's ole peeled plum-head into his mouth.

I don't care how often it's been done to you, nor how talented a cocksucker is, there's always something about that first contact that makes you gasp, inside if not outside. A "specialist" is hardly ever a good cocksucker, but he wasn't bad. He used his lips and teeth to inch downward until his nose was flattened against the wiry hair of my lower belly. My cockhead passed easily through the red ring of his back throat and came to rest against his throat wall. I held it there a moment and then put my hands flat over his ears. That had been done often enough to me so that I knew that the sounds of his world were shut off, and that he heard nothing except a seashell roaring. His eyes were squinched tight, leaving only his nose open — and his mouth, but it was full.

I deepened my voice somewhat and spoke louder so that he could hear. "All right, toesucker," I said. "Here's a bigger toe for you to work on. Gimme a first-class job, buddy."

He heard me, I'm sure, because he started a long slow job on me, withdrawing my cock almost to the head, then fluttering his tongue over the corona, seeking the underside of it to tickle and caress it, and wedging the point of his tongue into the slit, where I felt that a pearl of pre-come had formed. Then from somewhere inside, he created a vacuum, his cheeks hollowed with the great suction that he put on the length of my cock. And after that, his cheeks puffed out somewhat, so that instead of my cock being drawn into his mouth, I felt its being forced out — a very unusual sensation. He had one hand clamped tightly around the base of ole Betsy; I knocked it away, and then noticed that with his right hand he was jacking himself off as he kneeled in front of me.

I looked in the mirror, seeing that my knees were slightly bent, my ass tight, my midsection curved forward and out, and his own back and shoulder muscles moving in a pattern that was very pleasing. So, still looking in the mirror, still with my hands over his ears, I suddenly held his head immobile and stopped his up-and-down swallowings. Then I slowly started to fuck his mouth, long punishing thrusts, giving him hardly time to breathe between them. I was undecided whether to look down at my young pleasure-giver or sidewise into the mirror.

23

And then there suddenly began, deep in my groin, the old familiar thrills awakening. They rippled and rippled like a soft lapping of feather-soft fires, mounting to specks of brilliance. In the mirror I saw all my muscles tensed and hardened. The feeling was exquisite; I felt all my insides melting, and thought that I could really hear the tinklings of the nerve ends opening. It was as if my flesh were expanding, calling out for something. Strangely new rhythmic contractions swelled and swelled inside me, while my whole body seemed to be slipping round and round the sides of a deepening whirlpool of heat and liquid. Sensation in waves swirled and swept through my body, deeper and deeper, and then began the electric fingerings in my loins and legs, while the orderings of my system fled up to my brain, registered, and swept back to my cock. I looked one final time in the mirror, saw my neck corded, my head thrown back, every muscle hardened and shadowed under the ceiling light, and came in his mouth, pressing his face and head close against my belly, conscious only of the strength of my spurting into his deep throat as my gyzym filled his mouth and choked him, making him gag until the contractions of his throat muscles were cruel against my sensitized cock.

"My god!" I said, straightening my body. Just then I felt a hot splash against my feet and ankles. Jim had come. I looked down and saw a white flood sliding slowly, thickly, down over my feet.

I released his head, letting out a great *whoosh!* and swatted Jimmyboy playfully alongside his crewcut head. "Damn, boy," I said. "If you're that good at cocksuckin', it's a shame you're so hungup on feet. You'd make a million with that mouth and throat of yours."

He looked up, smiled a little, and then looked at my feet again, covered with semen, already beginning to thin somewhat and run toward the floor.

"D'you mind?" he murmured, and then without waiting for an answer bent his head and with a flattened tongue

24

licked my ankles and arches, even getting as far as he could between the toes. I kept my feet flat on the floor, looking down at his moving head. Finally he finished, and looked up the length of my body.

"Satisfied?" I asked, running my hand through his crewcut.

He nodded. "More to the point," he said, "are you?"

"More than," I said.

"I just wanted to mix mine with yours," he said, smiling, and laid his hand flat against his belly.

"That'll make you pregnant . . . maybe," I laughed.

"I wouldn't mind."

He got to his feet and put his arms briefly around my waist. I tensed, and pushed him away a little with my hand against his chest.

"Okay, Mac," I growled. "I won't say I didn't enjoy it, because I did. But let's not get sloppy. Sex's sex."

"Yeah," he said, and stepped back. He pulled on his pants. I turned to the washbowl, lifted my foot up into it and washed off the residue of his gyzym, then my other foot and finally my cock. He was dressed when I turned around.

"Jerry'll give you the twenty," he said.

I shook my head. "Business is business, too," I said. "You get it from him and then give it to me."

His mouth twitched in a half-grin. "What'sa matter? Don't you trust him?"

"With all but my grandmaw's jeweled bedpan," I said. "But let's keep it that way. The sucker pays the suckee in this house."

"I'm gonna mark this down as a red-letter day on my calendar," Jim said. "Four feet and one cock."

"It was damned good, kiddo," I said.

He opened his mouth, working his tongue, and after a moment pulled out a single hair. "I'll keep this," he said.

I picked up a small pair of scissors from the shelf above the washbowl. "Not enough," I said. "You'll lose it." I reached down to my crotch and pulled a curl out to its full length, from the hair right beside my cock, and snipped it off.

I handed it to him. His eyes glowed. "Put that in your memory book," I said.

"You betcha I will. I'll chew on it when I'm old and grey."

I opened the door. He pinched the pubic hair tightly between thumb and forefinger.

"So long, stud," he said. "For the moment. Can I do it again?"

"Any time," I said. And then, poking my tongue sardonically into my cheekwall, I said, "You can bring the twenty to me before I take a nap."

He didn't know it, but the way he sucked cock, he could have had it for nothing.

3. The Cat's Away

The next morning Jerry said to me, "I gotta go to Los Angeles this afternoon. How's about answerin' the phone for a coupla days and making all the arrangements for the guys?"

"You goin' down to meet your smut-angel?"

Jerry made a wry face. "I'm runnin' out of money," he said. "Hardly enough left to buy another hundred feet of film. Yeah, I gotta see him. I'll give you thirty-five a day to mind the store."

Then it was my turn to make a face. "'Spose I want to go out on a call myself?"

Jerry grinned. "Then the whole amount's yours," he said. "You'd keep it anyway."

"You bastard," I said, and took a mock swing at him.

He ducked, laughing. "Naw," he said. "I know you'd turn it in. But if I say you can keep it, then I don't have to worry. Besides," he said, "you're the only one around here except Teddy who's got sense enough to answer the phone."

"You mean, don'tcha, sense enough to weed out the kooks and the fuzz from the legit customers."

"Yeah," Jerry said.

"Is Teddy going?"

"No," he said. "And listen . . . you keep your hands off him, or I'll scratch your eyes out."

"You nut," I said, "you know I don't go for chicken."

"All of seventeen and a half," Jerry said stoutly.

"Still chicken," I said.

". . . and very mature in the head," Jerry said.

"But not in the eyes of our sovereign state," I said. "Hell . . . he really is a bouncy kid. The world's hardly made a dent in him yet. Seems too bad he'll have to change."

" 'Shades of the prison house begin to close'. . ." Jerry said, and I finished ole Wordsworth's quote: " 'around the growing boy.' "

"If he grows any more in front," Jerry grumbled, "I'm gonna have to get me a set of Doctor Young's rectal dilators."

I'd seen them once. Three-inch black hard-rubber, flanged at the end, graduated in size from the diameter of your little finger to that of a parlor-sized cock—modern America's answer to the graduated wooden pegs of the East Indian male bordellos. But today we had our own stretchers, pink plastic pricks.

"So that's what you and the kid do in bed, mother," I said, sardonic.

"We do everything," Jerry said.

"S/M too?"

"Naw . . . not that."

"Then not everything," I said. "What's he see in you anyway? Father image?"

"I'm not all that old. Thirty. And you're twenty-nine."

"Me a father image for him too, huh?" I said with a grin.

"As I said, I'll scratch your eyes out," Jerry said.

"Don't worry, little father. I wouldn't touch him for anything."

So Jerry left, and from that afternoon for the next two days I was more or less in charge.

There's nothing worse than the boredom that comes to a hustlers' house when you have a few slack days. True, there was a little action. Davey went out twice and I went out once; Pete got one call and a cowboy named Tex got two. Teddy and myself screened the calls, being careful that, despite the fact that Jerry advertised openly and at length in the gay newspapers, the "client" who telephoned was always able to mention someone whom either Teddy or I knew personally. That way you avoided the fuzz, who were just then getting wise to the fact that they could entrap anyone from Jerry's stable by renting a room in a hotel and pretending to want one of his "models." So the telephone conversations were really the sensitive part of the thing. By inflection, word usage, reference to a former client, knowledge of the lingo, and all those hundred little details that make up a kind of recognition code, we had to be able to separate the sheep from the fuzz. There was no trouble of any kind.

Except boredom. Hustlers aren't the most intelligent people in the world, by and large, nor do they have enough inner resources to fall back on when they're alone. I sometimes wondered what would happen in America if a four-day week came about. Just how would the beer-guzzling, TV-watching, baseball-talking boobs spend all that leisure time? Three-day weekends were bad enough: everybody hopped in his car and tore off some place, just to get away from it all, and got killed in nice satisfying population-reducing numbers on the highways.

Man's a chaser, after women, other men, good times (in his mind), horses, sports—the list is long. And if he could only realize that there's one way to give himself the greatest activity known, sitting alone in his room and just thinking, he'd be happier. Thinking, that is, provided he's got enough material stored up inside to think with.

The hustlers didn't. Bored to death between calls, they looked at comic books, drank beer, talked on the telephone, yawned, and slept. Jerry had tried to get them interested in games—cards, things like Monopoly, darts—all no use. They were bored because they were empty. Hardly one of them could read without pain, without moving his lips to form the words; they crept from line to line like wounded snails. It was only the passive entertainment of TV that kept them alive. And so, slack-jawed, glassy-eyed, brainpans empty, they sat in front of the boobtube and let others do their "thinking" for them. I suppose they were actually no different from eighty-five percent of the straight male population of America. Or the female, for that matter . . .

The second evening of Jerry's absence, three or four of the models/masseurs/escorts were in the living room watching TV when I went through on my way to the bathroom to take a leak. The door to the john was about a foot ajar, and I didn't know if anyone was inside. I knocked with my knuckle on the paneling.

"Yeah?" It was Teddy's voice.

"Oh . . . sorry. I thought nobody—"

"C'mon in," Teddy said, and I pushed the door open all the way. He had just finished a shower and was drying a leg, one foot up on top of the john, his cock hanging down in a considerably larger dimension than I had ever been aware he had. He saw me looking at it.

"And here all the time I bet you thought I was just a kid," he said wryly.

I rested my butt against the edge of the washbowl. "Well, aren't you?"

"Hell, no," he said, vigorously toweling his hair.

"Be sure to dry behind your ears," I said sardonically.

He dropped the towel and sprang to the middle of the small room, his elbow brushing my T-shirt as he did. And then standing there, he struck a pose—a kind of humorously exaggerated bodybuilder's stance, twisting half sidewise, drawing one arm up to show his biceps, tightening the other against his side. "There!" he said triumphantly. "I still look like a kid?"

In truth, he didn't. He had the excellently developed thighs, back, and belly of a full adult, and the tension under which

30

he had placed his muscles made them stand out beautifully in the light from the overhead bulb, which caught every ridge and underlined it with shadow. All I could think of was a young Greek athlete at the exercise grounds, naked, gleaming with oil—or, in Teddy's case, the natural shine of a young and healthy body.

Then he broke the pose and turned his back toward me, interlacing his fingers behind his head, and wiggled his buttocks and whole body in a takeoff of a belly dancer's motions. He turned his head, grinning mischievously over his shoulder, and looked at me. "Howja like to get in there, daddy?"

"You goddamned little flirt!" I growled, but I grinned too. Then, pretending a calm I did not exactly feel, I stepped toward the toilet and unbuttoned my fly to take my cock out for a piss.

"You're the last person around here I'd touch. Jerry would slice my balls off."

He jumped a coupla feet and stood beside me, his whole body in motion, grinning up at me, hair damp, eyes sparkling. "Not if I didn't tell him anything, he wouldn't."

He laid a hand on my arm and with the other reached into my open fly. "Lemme hold it while you piss," he said.

Amused despite myself at his bounciness and youth, I folded my arms across my T-shirt and said, "Go ahead."

A little of his cockiness left him and he seemed uncertain. But he reached into my crotch, his hand warm and damp, and closed his fingers around ole Betsy, who—independent as she was, living her own life—immediately awakened.

"Man," Teddyboy breathed, "you can get a hardon quicker'n anybody I ever saw."

"All the better to screw you with, m'boy," I murmured. "Evidently you ain't seen many."

"Enough . . . daddy," he said, and his voice broke a little.

He had my cock entirely out now and it was half-hard. But he wasn't satisfied. His fingers went on digging until he had my balls out too. Then he closed his fist firmly around my cock. "Now piss," he said, his eyes on its head, which had deepened in color and grown considerably larger.

"You expect me to piss with a hardon? That's kinda difficult to do," I said.

"Try," he urged.

It took a coupla moments of concentration. I'd been drinking some beer, and really had to take a leak, god knows, but the hand around my cock, and the other hand on my shoulder, tended to stop me. Finally I thought, oh, what the hell, and the stream began. He guided it right into the center of the pool where it made a hell of a racket.

Meanwhile, my hyperkinetic little friend watched and watched. I cast a look at his cock; it had risen and was fully hard. He was not circumcised, but the expanding head had forced the foreskin back. It was a big one, all right. I smelled the fragrant masculine soap he'd used on his hair, felt his naked body pressing against my forearm and thigh.

Then I finished. Teddy milked the last drops, shook my cock as if it were his own, and started to tuck it back inside. Despite the fact that I'd just taken a leak, I was by no means soft and flaccid, but in that intermediate stage when your cock seems to weigh a coupla pounds and is heavy and swollen with residual blood. Teddy was still tucking it away, his lips dry. He moistened them with his tongue, and finally got ole Betsy back in the stall.

"Lissen," he said, grabbing my upper arm with a strong grip. His voice told me something. The banter was gone; the timbre was low, resonant, and husky. "I really do want you."

"Aw, come off it," I growled. "I can't, on account of Jerry. You just don't do this sort of thing when you're in a guy's stable, living in his house and eating his food."

"The hell you don't," Teddy said. "I know you. You're a sensualist. You'd fuck anything, even a knothole in a wooden fence. I told you I wouldn't tell. And lissen, man . . . I'm good."

"What's the matter with you?" I growled. "You really got a father hangup? You stretch it a little, or have me born in Tennessee, and I'm almost old enough to *be* your father."

"I . . . don't think it's . . . that," he said slowly. "I think it's a matter of experience. I kinda look through you, if you know what I mean, and see all that long line of studs you've been with. And in having you fuck me, it's like . . . well . . ."

". . . like having a coupla thousand fuck you at once?" I finished.

"That's it," he said. "You kinda got a dark . . . sorta mysterious past. And you're smart . . . intelligent. I wish I'd been through all you've been through."

"Oh, no, you don't," I said, faintly bitter.

"Well, part of it," he said. His naked arms slipped around me. "C'mon, will yuh?"

You cover it with lots of old clichés, such as a stiff prick knows no conscience, or wears blinders, or some such. Too much experience erodes your ethics, if you ever had any. In spite of the whole situation, I found my arms going around his naked body, felt his trembling and his desire. I drew him close to me. One of my hands caressed the small of his back, slipping slowly lower until my fingers felt the beginning of the crack between those exciting small muscular cheeks, lightly covered with a sprinkling of his dark-brown hair. My hand crept down, and with my fingers I slowly parted the cheeks of his ass—it was damper inside—and located the little puckerhole, and pushed.

His groin pushed harder against mine. "Please, Phil," he said, his voice muffled in my armpit, his head close against my chest.

The young seduce the old, by God. Still holding him, my finger pushing at his asshole, I put my other hand under his chin and forced his head up so that I could look him in the eyes. They were enormous, lust-filled, brown flecked with green.

"What about Jerry?" I asked softly.

"The cat's away," he said, and grinned. "I swear I'll never tell."

"It'd be sticky if you did," I said. "For both of us." Oh, Wilde was so right when he said you could resist anything except temptation!

He leaned farther back and with one hand made a gesture at his smooth chest. "Cross my heart," he said. "Scout's honor and all that crap."

"Really and honestly?"

"I'd never squeal," he said firmly. "I'm my own man, goddamnit, and nobody owns me. I ain't no damn heifer. No concubine."

I ruffled his hair, remembering the two times Jerry and I had made the scene together. "You're a damn cute kid," I said, "and smart too. And handsome. If you wanta be fucked . . . let's go."

The delight that showed in his face, the mixture of lust and pleasure, was rewarding. He buried his face against my chest and then released me, dancing excitedly, glowing. "Your room or mine?"

"Mine, ninny. You're not supposed to be one of the whores. If anyone hears anything in my room they'll leave us alone. And nobody ever comes in if you're with a score."

"Okay," he said and grabbed my hand, leading me down the corridor. From the TV room some cunt was blatting a nasal country-western song. We got inside number seven and I closed the door, turning on the small rosy fucklight.

"I wanta undress you," he said excitedly, one strong young hand pushing me towards the bed. The edge of it caught me behind the knees and I fell back, catching myself and resting on my elbows.

"Okay, buster," I said. "Boots first."

He was standing in front of me, his cock hard and swollen, sticking straight out from his lower belly. Then I noticed something. Interested, I put my index finger out and touched its red head, pushing it down a little. Released, the cock bobbed back up, and then, wonder of wonders, went on bobbing like a postal scale, perfectly balanced, nodding up and down like the head of those mandarin china figures that go on and on, with a spring hidden in the neck.

"I'll be damned," I said. "Never saw a prick like that."

He laughed. "Shows how well-balanced I am, huh?" Then he got on his knees between my widespread legs, tugging at my right boot, which came off easily along with the sock. Then he got the other one. He took that foot in his hand, cupping the heel in his palm, and looked at it speculatively.

"Does a toejob feel as good to everybody as Jim's did to me yesterday?"

"Almost," I said, "except the ticklish ones. They can't stand it."

"Being tickled is a form of pain, ain't it?" he asked.

I was astounded. Out of the mouths of babes, etc. Without ever reading Freud or Stekel (I presumed), the kid had intuitively hit on the truth.

"Sure," I said.

"Do you like it?"

"Love it," I said. "But some other time. Right now I want to spread the cheeks of that nice little fig."

He laughed. "Unplucked so far," he said.

"Hah, I'll bet!" I said.

"Stand up, will yuh?" he asked.

I got off the bed. He pulled at my T-shirt and I raised my arms over my head so that he could get it off. He did, and dropped it on the floor, lowering his face to brush his cheek across my mat of black hair, and then he found my trigger, my right nipple, and drew it into his mouth. For my cock that was the bell for the curtain, ending the intermission.

"C'mon, buddy," I said. "Let's get crackin'. Down to business."

He unfastened my chinos, and slid them down. Ole Betsy came out with a bump and stood up against my belly, and then suddenly he was all over me, his mouth wide open, kissing and sucking and lapping, tongue sometimes flat and sometimes pointed to get into my navel, slipping sidewise down in the tender secret places of my crotch at the side of my balls, bending double to plant a big sloppy smack on the arches of my feet, then standing again, and grabbing me to him. Long he hugged me, long and close — to quote Whitman.

"Kiddo," I said. "Look at it. It's ready."

He closed his fingers around my cock, and moved his hand back and forth slowly.

"How do you want it?" I asked. "What position?"

Somewhat timidly he said, "Can I sit on it the way Davey did a coupla days ago?"

"Whatever turns you on," I said.

I lay down on the bed lengthwise and he straddled me, surprising me that he faced my feet, not my head. But that was nice. It gave me a wonderful view of the excellently muscled terrain of his back, darkened with the early summer sun, muscled like a weightlifter's. He straddled my groin on his knees, his feet just touching my armpits, and reached around behind. In his hurry he had forgotten to use any grease, but not I. The big jar of Perfection cold cream sat open on the night-table; I dipped a coupla fingers in it and hit him with it between his cheeks. He gasped faintly at the coolness. And then I spread the rest of it on my cock and slyly wiped my hand on the sheet at the side of the bed.

He got hold of the middle of my cock and guided it towards his asshole, lodging the head of it in the slippery gobbet. There was an indrawn breath, and then, using the leverage of his hard young thigh muscles, he began to sink slowly down, pausing when he reached the sphincter. At least he'd been around the house long enough to know approximately what to do; there was no necessity to give him physiological instructions like "Higher! Lower! There!" as you often had to do with complete amateurs.

I could see a thin sweat now on his back; my cockhead was evidently a bit large for him. His legs, which had clasped my

36

ribcage tightly, now moved outward, spreading the cheeks of his ass. Balancing on the hot-point, he reached around behind and pulled his cheeks apart, a thing I should have done for him. I reached down, pushed his hands away and sank my thumbs deeply into his asscheeks, my fingers on his pelvic bones, pulling the cheeks well apart and holding his body tightly just where it was. With almost imperceptible upward movements of my hips (oh, he felt them!), I nudged my cockhead gently against the inside ring and, slowly, like an infinitely expansible iris, it began to open.

He knew it, and with a sigh sank slowly down. I watched my cock go in, until his firm and widespread cheeks flattened my pubic hair, and he was sitting close and heavy upon me.

Now it was my turn. With fingertips and then with flattened palms, I caressed his back, his cheeks and thighs as far as I could reach. Then raising a little, I reached around for his hardened young nipples, rolling them between thumb and forefinger, and finally slowly pulled his body backward against me.

He sighed again and with an upward motion of his body unbent his knees, stretching his legs down partly on mine, partly to the side. He was not squarely on top of me, but angled slightly to the right side.

It was a good position. I began a slow rotating motion of my hips, one I knew would send my cock first right, then left, poking into all the secret spots of his asshole. His sighing now was almost continuous, and then gradually changed character, a kind of low keening, almost guttural, ending in small gasps, pleasure sounds if ever I heard them.

The whole fuck was wordless. It was as if it had been choreographed, a sexual ballet. We pressed against each other, never breaking connection. After a few minutes of the pleasure of fucking him from underneath, I rolled him over on his left side, and then went on—slow sometimes, often drawing my cock nearly out, poking at the rim of the chalice (a new series of sounds from him, almost muffled yelps), and then back deep again. Slowly I pushed my knees against the backs of his, nudging them upward.He took the cue, drawing his legs up into an almost fetal position, while with my right hand on top of his hipbone I again pulled a cheek wide. This time I went clear in—long slow ones, followed by a series of half-strokes, very rapid.

And after that, with his legs still drawn up, I rolled on top of him, his knees bent under him in genuflection, prostrate, his head resting on the bed and his ass in the air. I looked down. The grease had spread until the cheeks of his butt glistened in the rosy light, and my cock glinted along all its length. And in and out, in and out, sometimes slow, sometimes fast. I was enjoying it tremendously. From his small animal sounds, I think he was too.

It was beginning to get to me. The walls of his ass tunnel seemed to grow hotter, and I speeded my movements until the rapidity of my thrusts created a kind of engine sound, like a well-greased piston plunging in its cylinder and withdrawing with a sound of suction. And then suddenly, with no warning, with none of the lovely preliminaries I usually felt—there it was! Spasm after spasm, my whole body was contracting in convulsive shudders. I hardly remember what I did. I bent over him, clutching him tightly around his belly and reaching for his cock, jacking him off in time with my slowing thrusts, and then feeling him arch his ass until his cockhead was in my palm. With frantic movements of his body he ground his cock into my hand, and I felt it fill with heat and liquid, felt the violent shuddering of his body and the contractions of his cock as his gyzym slid slowly through my fingers.

Without any signaling I withdrew and turned on my back. He lay on his side, nose in my armpit. We were both panting.

I let out a great lungful of air. "Oh, man!" I said. "What a way to go."

His breathing was still quick and deep. "Did . . . you . . . like it?" he gasped.

"One of the best," I said, "of all the thousands."

"I'm glad," he said, snuggling against my side. Then he said, "I'll tell you a secret if you won't tell."

"Scout's honor," I said, laughing.

"Y-You . . . got my cherry."

I sat bolt upright. "You're kiddin'!"

He shook his head, grinning. "I would never let Jerry . . . or anybody . . . get it. I . . . I wanted the best . . . breaking-in."

"I'm flattered," I said. "But you did it like an old pro. How come?"

He laughed. "I've lived in this house for two years," he said. "And I've kept my ears and eyes open."

". . . and now your asshole," I said.

"Yup. You might call it on-the-job training. Haven't you ever heard of a mechanic learning to use his tools just by watchin' his fellow workers?"

"You're no mechanic," I said. "You're one of those rare birds . . . a natural-born expert."

"I like you too," he said happily, and buried his nose deeper into my armpit, snuggling close.

4. A Sothron Stud

Jerry was back from Los Angeles right when he said he would be, and all went as before. I did not feel particularly guilty that I had been poaching on his territory. I knew that Teddy's span of living with Jerry was limited, for Jerry tired of his *mignons*, his little darlings, easily. At the age of thirty, he had already had Great Affairs with sixteen of them. And I knew enough of the homosexual life to realize that the butterfly syndrome affected us all, that sooner or later these protestations of undying love weakened, for one partner always loved less than the other. Nothing was permanent in our hummingbird world; the pastures were always greener, etc. By eye or gesture and finally by act, a person in a homosexual liaison finally gave way. I did not have to rationalize my fucking Teddy; he wanted it, I gave it to him, and if he had any remorse for his action, he could have comforted himself by investigating. He would have found Jerry had been unfaithful to him at least a dozen times in the two years they had been together. I could personally vouch for at least two of those occasions.

The evening of his return, I found him alone in the living room, thinking. The TV was on, but the sound had been turned off. He was sitting on the black leather sofa, which an angry hustler had once carved to ribbons with a razor blade when he thought Jerry had been cheating him.

"You, man," I said, "seem to be deep in thought, as they say."

He looked up. "I am," he said. He patted the sofa. "Siddown."

I sat. "I got the money okay," he said, "enough to finish the picture. But I'm havin' trouble with the story line. Lissen," he said, turning towards me, and laying on me that Earnest Look of his friendly brown eyes which always indicated he wanted something. "You're a smart cookie . . . Ohio State grad and all that, though I never could understand why you took up hustlin'—"

I smirked. "I'm a great humanitarian," I said, "a philanthropist," and he groaned at the high-level pun on my name, "who wants to bring pleasure and happiness to lonely old men in their hotel rooms at night. But you were talkin' about your own troubles . . ."

"Yeah," he said. "How's about your helpin' me with the script? You could take three, four episodes from your past, and sketch out a little dialogue . . ."

"I ain't never done nuthin' like that," I growled.

Jerry grinned at me. "Oh, c'mon now," he said. "You can drop the dumb hustler talk with me. I know more about you than you think."

So I grinned in return. "Okay, *mon ami*," I said. "What's in it for me?"

"Well," he said. "I'll lay a coupla hundred on you for some dialogue and script, and then if the thing goes well, I'll cut you in for about ten percent of the net . . ."

"Can we have that in writing?"

"Well, we'd have to see how that rides with the guy in L.A. who's financing the whole project, but the important thing is to get this film off the ground. I've had three films and they've all been pretty successful, pullin' in about twenty to thirty grand . . ."

"Jerry," I said firmly, "you slipped out of that one very neatly, but lemme tell you something. You know that crooked pornie publisher back east, that fuckin' albino . . .?"

He nodded. "Well," I went on, "he's got an international reputation for being a con-man and a crook in all his dealings, so much so that nobody'll have anything to do with him any more. And as a friend, I'll have to say it, you're rapidly approaching his reputation as the leading double-dealer here on the West Coast. Now . . ." I said, seeing the storm clouds gather, "how about answering my question? Can we have that in writing?"

One thing about an accomplished operator: he knows how and when to bend with the wind. Jerry's frown was erased, and he grinned. "Sure you can, Phil," he said. "You want it right now?"

"Naw," I said, stretching my legs. "Later." Mistake number one.

"And think of the publicity you'll get if there's a movie about you," he continued excitedly, "using your own name and face."

"Yeah," I said. Mistake number two. "I can double my rates."

Well, two hundred wasn't much, but I still was not one to sneeze in its direction. The ten percent interested me more, but despite his assurances I had a kind of gut feeling that there'd be a high wind in Jamaica before I saw any of it.

Jerry took hold of my right thigh and squeezed, and then patted it. "Okay, man," he said. "You do a little thinking about it, will yuh? Then we'll talk."

"How soon you want it?" I asked.

"Soon as possible," he said. "Yesterday. Looks like we're gonna have another coupla days of rain, and we can't shoot until it stops. See what you can do."

"Sure thing," I said and unfolded myself from the sofa, stretching my arms wide and yawning. "I think I'll take a nap. I do my best thinking then."

42

"Okay," Jerry said, and I left him to his meditation.

On the way to my room I passed number five, inhabited by a guy we called Tex, or Tex-ass. No one knew his real name. He was a tall, lean, really skinny dude, ugly as a camel and towheaded, with a face that just didn't seem to fit together—nose too long, chin too short, and ears that would make him take off in a high wind. His costume was a cowboy hat and denim jeans and jacket, with a red bandanna looped around his corded neck. All in all, not the handsomest one in the stable, but he was there for another reason. He had the biggest cock west of the Mississippi, a long stiff ramrod that appealed to all the size queens in San Francisco. When he paraded the streets—as he seldom did, because his telephone popularity kept him from cruising—it was a caution to the jaybirds. Full, thickly dangling, pendant, his cock hung down his left leg well below the halfway mark, and it was all he could do to stuff it and his hen's-egg balls into the matchstick jeans he wore. He'd been married four times (see your friendly neighborhood psychiatrist, please) and shacked up God knows how often, and not even he knew how many little bastards of his were runnin' around Texas in the vicinity of Fort Worth. And no one knew, either, why he was hustling in San Francisco—and no one asked, following the rules of the game.

His door was partly open and I sneaked a look. He was lying on his side completely naked, legs partly drawn up. His top half was deeply tanned; from the waist down he was perfectly white. The contours of his small ass were relaxed, but even so the cheeks were hollowed with his wiry musculature. I decided I wouldn't mind seein' his frontside again. Everybody, even straights, was fascinated by an oversized cock.

"How's my ole buddy Tex-ass?" I asked softly.

He wasn't asleep. He turned his head back to look at me. "Oh, hiya, Phil," he said. "C'mon in. Ah wuz jes' restin' a mite."

"Have a hard night?"

"Jes' one score," he drawled, "but by jiminy I wisht I dint. I'm outta business for at least a coupla days."

"How come?"

He raised up on his elbows. "Jes' look at the gol-durned thing," he said mournfully. "I got me a john las' night and I reckon I wuz too much for him, account he done scraped and scratched me sumpin' fierce. Look," he said, and put two fingers under the heavy limp thing he called his cock. It was streaked with red in four or five places, and there were several black and blue marks on it.

I whistled. "Sheez!" I said. "What was he tryin' to do . . . get it ready for a barbecue?"

"It wuz too goddamned big for him," Tex said sadly. "He shoulda had false teeth."

"That cock oughta be stuffed and mounted," I said. "Or given to the Smithsonian."

"Huh?" he asked, blankly.

I waggled my hand. "Given to a museum," I said. "I should think that when it got hard you'd likely faint, what with all that blood rushin' down from your head."

He had no sense of humor. Correction: he had no sense. "Naw," he said, "that ain't ever happened to me. But this makes me goddamned mad. Ah cain't do a thing, and Ah'm horny as hell."

I sat down on the edge of the bed. "You could at least go out with somebody who wanted to cornhole you," I said.

"It's purty hard for me," he said. "Ah cain't come that way, usual."

I laughed. "Bet I could make you come like that."

"Fuckin' me, yuh mean?"

"Yeah."

"Without nobuddy a-touchin' it?"

"Yeah," I said.

"Okay . . . yer on," he said. "Betcha five."

"Done," I said.

He swung his long thin legs off the bed and went to the

44

door and closed it. Despite his injuries, the idea of getting fucked affected him a little; his cock arced out and downward more than it had when he came back to the bed.

"This I gotta see," he said.

"You'll not only see it . . . you'll feel it," I said, unbuckling my boots and taking them off, leaving my socks on. I peeled down my chinos and stepped out of them, and shrugged out of my leather jacket—no T-shirt at the moment. I looked down at my cock. Ole Betsy, god bless her, had grown aware of the situation and was sending me a little coded message, which when translated into clear text told me that I'd wanted to get into that tiny ass of Tex's for a long time. And what better way to spend a rainy afternoon in San Francisco?

"How you gonna?" he asked. "Back, side, belly?"

"First I gotta find out where your joyspot is," I said. I dipped a finger into the open pound jar of Perfection cold cream and got some all over my middle finger.

"You bend over and rest your elbows on the bed," I said, "whilst I do me a little investigatin'."

He did. His ass was smooth as marble, just as white and nearly as hard. There was a little hair growing down into the crack from the small of his back, but the cheeks themselves were perfectly smooth. My cock was fully hard in anticipation.

I touched my finger to the puckerhole, rosy-brown in the exposed crack. "Spread your feet a bit," I said, and he did.

His asshole drew in on itself at my touch, but he made no other sign. Then very slowly I advanced my finger, finding it blocked by a very tight sphincter. I pushed gently against it, small pushes, several times, and in about thirty seconds I felt it open. My finger went in as far as it could, exploring.

It took no time at all to find his prostate. It was dead-on and low-set. I stroked it with the ball of my finger, and then on the other side with the flat of my nail. This time he did gasp, and wiggled his ass a little.

"Godalmighty!" he said. "That shore feels good."

"Just wait, kiddo," I said, "until I really get goin'."

I withdrew my finger and toweled it, and then checked the angle at which it had gone in. "Lower your ass a little," I said. "Bend your knees."

I dipped into the jar again and spread a generous amount on ole Betsy. It was steel-hard now, and the head of it nearly violet with the savage blood. I bent my knees a bit, too, so that the angle of penetration would be the same as my finger, and then I gently touched the tip of my cock to his asshole, sending a series of small pushes behind it.

He jumped forward slightly, and his body flinched. "Y'all take it easy now, y'hear?" he said. "Please?"

"Sure thing," I said.

Well, I thought, *with a cock like that in front, big enough to pull him down stoop-shouldered, you could easily understand why his asshole hadn't been used much.* Life settles down to being a choice of pleasures, I reckon. Still, it was too bad the size of his cock automatically cut him out of half of life's experiences.

"Ummh," he grunted. My pushing against his asshole had had some small reward. I felt the head slip in, at first just about a half-inch, and then, continuing the pressure with a flexing and relaxing of my knees, I felt the whole cockhead enter.

"Ow," he said.

I patted his smooth white-marble ass, and ran my fingers over the hollows made by the strong muscle, and at the same time went on pushing gently.

"Just take it easy, ole buddy," I said. "I've ridden as many assholes as you've ridden horses. I ain't gonna kill you."

Then I eased my cockhead through the first sphincter. His head came up like a bronc's, but this time he didn't holler. The small vestibule just inside his asshole cupped the head of my cock tightly. And it was hot! The enclosure, the strong ring of flesh, was tight as a teenager's. It pressed close against my cockhead, so firmly that ole Betsy, with that independent will of her own, throbbed three or four times with the sensation, almost as if she were ready and eager to come right now.

"I ain't gonna hurry this here up," I said softly. "We'uns want y'all to have fun, hey?" Unconsciously I slipped into an imitation of his speech, the same way I would have with a real score.

"Y'all ain't gonna take too long, Ah hope," he said.

"Nope," I said.

I braced myself on my tightened leg muscles and grabbed the sides of his slim hips with my outspread fingers. Beneath the sinewy muscles I could feel the hard and enduring pelvic bones. I dug my fingers into the cheeks of his ass (not a blemish on it!) and pulled them even wider apart.

You had to handle this bronc carefully, so I started long and slow. My cockhead, stimulated and strongly gripped as it was, went slowly in, tingling every centimeter of the way. As a connoisseur of assholes, I was ready to say that ole Tex-ass had about the hottest, tightest tunnel I'd ever let a ray of light into. I felt my way like a blind one-eyed explorer through the narrow crevice until I bumped gently against his prostate.

That was it. I set the lantern down and went to work. Using the circular fulcrum of his asshole, I sent ole Betsy deep inside, brushing first against the right side of his joyspot, then poking it dead center, and then grazing it again on the left side as I came out.

"By . . . damn," Tex said between gasps, "that shore feels mighty purty, man." And then he went back to breathing hard against the bedspread, his homely face turned sidewise. There was sweat on his forehead.

"Glad you like it, man," I said. I was cool and objective about it, and still enjoying it a lot. The muffled moaning in Tex's throat was a reward much better than the five-dollar bet — which I knew I'd win. He kept turning his head from side to side.

After about three minutes of that massaging, I started a different motion, bending up and down on my toes while I pushed in and out, knowing that such a movement now was getting the top and the bottom of his joyspot instead of the sides. His moaning increased, and a fine luster of sweat began to glisten on his back. His cock was up against the side of the bed now (it was so big it could never stand up against his belly because its weight dragged it downward), and he started to fuck the bed, forward and back. That spoiled my carefully contrived rhythm until I adjusted to it and then went relentlessly on.

But at the same time, nonparticipating as I had thought myself to be, something was beginning to happen. I looked down at my cock, traveling thick and inflamed into his asshole, glistening with grease. I began to enjoy myself.

And then suddenly with no warning, a fantasy sprang into my head—a memory, really—of the wild days with handsome young Bull at Lake McDonald hotel in Glacier Park, and old Angus, the foreman of the packsaddle trips, and his bunch of ornery leathery tough cowboys who acted as tourist guides. And especially of the one night when all of us had got drunk after a dance in the rec hall, and gone to sit around a real honest-to-god campfire, while Angus spun his drunken yarns for the tourists, and we all kept passing the bottle around. And then one by one the tourists went back to bed, with only stalwart young Bull and myself left among the cowboys. That was the night I had been surprised—even shocked, back in those golden lost days—when Bull, my roommate, my very butch roommate, had suddenly jumped into the middle of the campfire with his boots, scattering but not extinguishing it, and started to pull down his pants, hollering "I wanna be fucked!" at the top of his voice.

And we were all only too glad to oblige . . . old Angus first, and a half-dozen cowpokes after him, and myself as Bull's roommate last, all of us fucking him in his muscular young nineteen-year-old ass as he lay on the grass under the arch of the night sky, while the stars wheeled around the black vault above. I had seen more cowboys' asses that night, their lean hips pumping in the flickering shadows of the firelight, chaps and Levi's down around their ankles, their solid thighs and legs catching the glimmering of the campfire, than I had seen before or since.

I looked down at my cock, traveling into Tex's asshole, thinking that for a moment I saw a glint of firelight on it once again. Then I was back in the whorehouse on Mason Street, and Tex was moaning and twisting under me. I drew my cock nearly out so that I could admire the length of it, leaving a bare inch inside which I sent poking around the confined imprisoning cup of his ass tunnel.

"Aw, g'damn it!" Tex exploded. "Git it back in thar the same way! Ah'm ahbout ready to pop, man!"

And pop he did. The contractions on my cock were violent, nearly expelling ole Betsy from her second home. And the added squeezing did something for me—it sent me back to Montana, to the sight of Bull's white-marble ass, wet with a half-dozen loads from the cowpokes who'd fucked him, still moving and eager in the flickering half-light, and myself standing ready, cock in hand and hard, cheered on by the circle of drunken cowpokes, and then stretched out on Bull's moving body, feeling the gutsy thrill (increased by my going into the pool of hot, wet gyzym already deposited there in his asshole), the chilling ecstasy of the beginning of my own orgasm.

I collapsed on top of Tex's body, my hands underneath his chest, finding and rolling his nipples while I poured great gouts of my white gyzym-nectar into him (or Bull), bathing his battered prostate. He felt me come, and had sense enough to contract his hot tunnel gently, milking me of the day's first production. He kept saying "Oh, oh!" over and over. I was sweating and breathing hard, and so was he.

I stayed joined to him while he climbed up out of the deep well of what the Latins call the little death, and while our

49

blood pressures and breathing and pulsebeats came back to normal.

Then I slowly withdrew. He turned and looked at me, his homely face shiny with sweat. "Ah'll be gol-durned," he drawled. "Ah dint think it could be done."

"That'll be five bucks, man," I said, grinning.

"Ah'd be proud," he said. " 'N mebbe y'all'd do it agin, huh?"

"Anytime, man," I said. "I enjoyed it too. Next time . . . no bet. No charge. Professional courtesy."

"Huh?"

"Forget it," I said, doubling my fist and punching him lightly on the jawbone.

"Ah be damned," he said, slowly, thoughtfully. "Y'know, now Ah got me an idee how a woman feels. Why she likes fuckin' so much."

"It's give and take," I said. "You gotta know how to do it."

"Ifn y'all shows me sometime," he said slowly, "Ah reckon Ah'd double the number of scores Ah get. Usual, Ah just jump on and off, rabbitlike."

"We'll do it again sometime," I said. "I'll show you how."

"Ah'd be right proud," he said again, and there was a large grin on his plain face.

5. The Past Recaptured

It was very unusual weather for May in the San Francisco area, all the natives said. Rain. Usually the winter lasted about three or four weeks of more or less steady downfall, and then it was all over. The hills were green for a month or two, then started to turn brown, and stayed that way until the following year's rainy season. But this year was different. The rain had started in November and gone on and on, until the inch measurements had passed the double mark.

It hadn't affected the business of Jerry's stable at all; if anything, it had increased it. For what was better on a rainy afternoon than a good slow fuck with a warm and active body in bed?

The day after the conversation with Jerry and the good screw of Tex-ass, I lay on the bed—the workbench—in my room, door closed, listening to the eaves dripping and the water running heavy down the gutter drainpipes. I was in that pleasant half-state between waking and sleeping, but my mind, instead of drifting away, seemed to be more active than usual, as I tried to think back over fourteen years of hustling to pick out the episodes that seemed to me to be easiest for Jerry to handle in a low-budget movie.

But alas! there was an overabundance of them. If you're

51

one of those persons who live a completely sexual life, so much so that you can't even see the fork of a tree without thinking of it as the crotch of a man standing on his head, then you've really got too much to draw from instead of not enough.

Where to begin? In New York, Dallas, Chicago, Los Angeles, San Francisco? I thought idly of Larry Johnson, the deep-voiced stud who'd lived with me for a while in Berkeley, gradually changing from a street person into an Establishment member, and finally going so far as to sign up for the San Francisco Police Department. I thought of his treachery in listing me and twenty others in Berkeley for various "sex crimes" under the laws of the sovereign state of Califor-ni-ay, and of how I'd framed him by stashing some dope in the house before I left it, and writing a coupla notes to the Police Department in the City. Then I'd left in a hurry, and had sometimes wondered what had happened to him. The worst, I hoped. But next to my favorite fuzz, Greg Wolfson, I couldn't help liking Larry the most—so tall, so handsome and arrow-straight, arrogant and bossy, and the very best in bed. Well, better pull down the window shade on that.

But I couldn't stay away from San Francisco for long, even if it were a little dangerous for me. I could not live away from water. The city with its continental attitudes, the charm of its old houses and steep hills, had drawn me back within a coupla months. But was there a deeper reason? Was it the death-wish city, trembling on top of the San Andreas fault, waiting for the next big earthquake to send it sliding into the bay? Was it the Queen City of the West because so many homosexuals, secretly and subconsciously burdened with a sense of guilt, migrated to it the way the lemmings swam out to sea to drown? In the years since I'd first come to the city, the death toll of suicides from the Golden Gate Bridge had risen from about three hundred to nearly eight, and each year saw an increase over the year before.

Thinking of Larry led me to thinking of Rudolf Dax in

Chicago, the weight-lifter hustler (now a cop), the hetero narcissist whom I had once tricked into blowing me. He had handled his former tricks by passing them by, stony-faced and with no recognition—when he met them on the street in his uniform. If they called, he never called back. Rudolf might make an interesting segment.

And then there was Ace Hardesty, the black I'd been involved with in Dallas and later in Chicago, the gigantic (in more ways than one) college-educated stud who, when I two-timed him, had got me into a gang rape with a half-dozen of his black buddies, leaving me sore and out of business for a month, rearwise, that is. He'd make another good one.

But Jerry was a sentimentalist. You couldn't go too far out with him: no S/M, no variations. And what did a cold son-ofabitch like me know about sentiment? When had I ever fallen "in love"?

Well, there was one time I came damned close—with Kenny in Chicago, the naive farm-kid who'd come to the big wicked city to learn welding, so's he could go back downstate and repair farm machinery. How he'd reacted when he found out I was a hustler! But evil old Mike Schmidt had made him a hustler, too, and after a while, if I wanted to screw Kenny, I had to pay him myself.

Or the contacts made while I was a masseur at the Lincoln Baths in Chicago—little bald Mondrat, the college professor; Bob Fitsimmons, the best-known artist in the area; old Ben Thomas, judge and jurist; Mr. Bennett, a drifter hung up on blacks, especially the Muslim called Adam X, and the brief and agonizing period of actual slavery I'd gone through with the two of them. Then Duke, the wickedest and most talented of American composers. Or the Easter Kid, who came to San Francisco every Easter, a Ph.D. from Canada and Bermuda, and his line about Zen, and how I'd fucked him while he was tied to his motorcycle . . .

They came and went in my memory, hundreds of them,

53

then thousands, a moving frieze on a Greek temple, stepping down now and then into my life. Too many . . . I'd have to be more selective for Jerry, and then get to work on a little remembered dialogue, which wouldn't be too hard, considerin' I had almost total recall.

There was a knock on the door.

"Yup?" I hollered. "Come in."

It was bouncy Teddyboy. "Call for you," he said. "Says he knows you. He's at the Mark Hopkins. Name of Art Kain."

Art Kain! Hell, I'd tried to make him for months while we were both goin' to Ohio State, about eight years ago, and finally succeeded once. He was a big bohunk, son of a coal miner, and handsome as the rosy-fingered dawn.

"Y'know him?" Teddy asked.

"Do I ever," I said, swinging off the bed. "I made him once. Wonder how he ever found me after eight years?"

Teddy smirked. "Oh, everybody knows the Great Whore of Babylon," and then he skipped aside, ducking my swing at him, and laughing.

I went to the phone and said "Yeah?" in my deepest bass.

"Phil Andros?"

"Yup, and how's old Artie-baby after all these years?"

A deep laugh. "Dandy," he said. "I hear you've gone into a new line of work."

"Not so new," I said gruffly. "Who told you?"

"Don Hughes," he said, and I remembered Don, the first guy who'd ever given me money, back in the old Deshler-Wallick hotel in Columbus, Ohio. He'd been a vice-president then for a cash register company in Dayton, and I, a fifteen-year-old. We'd known each other a long time.

"He said you were tops," Art said.

"If he thought so a coupla years ago, he'd be surprised now," I growled.

He laughed. "Can you come over to the Mark for a drink?"

"It'll cost you thirty-five cents," I said.

"No sweat," he said. "Room 1224."

"Right now?"

"Yup."

"Be there in thirty minutes," I said. "Gotta take a quick shower."

"Don't," he said.

"Okay . . . make it twenty. I'll have to put on a suit. Can't make it into the Mark in a leather jacket and chinos and boots."

"I'd prefer the jacket," he said, "but I've learned to compromise."

"Okay, man," I said. "Be good to see you." I hung up the phone and went back fast to number seven. I sat on the bed and pulled off my boots and socks, then stripped down my chinos. I hated like hell these out-calls when I had to dress up.

I'd just got naked when I looked up and there was Teddy-boy, arms folded, leaning against the doorjamb. "An okay guy?" he asked.

"Sure," I said. "Old friend. Ex-coal miner from West Virginia."

"I envy you," Teddy said.

"Him or me?" I grinned at him, pulling on my black nylon socks. Then I got up and took my suit from the closet and laid it on the bed — very conservative dark blue — and pulled a white shirt and tie from the dresser.

"Him, I guess," Teddy said, his full lips a little parted. He ran the tip of his tongue over his upper lip.

"You know what that tongue movement means in Europe?"

"No, what?" he asked.

"That you want sex of some kind," I said.

"I do, man, I do," he said softly because Jerry was back in the living room.

"Some of these days," I said, getting into my pants and shirt.

"Promise?" Teddy said.

"Next time Jerry goes outa town," I said, putting a thick knot in my tie. Then I put on my black shoes and stood up

"Gotta run now."

"Sure."

I got a plastic raincoat from the closet, goosed Teddy in the ass as I passed him, but he was quick, and returned the compliment by cupping his strong young hand over my cock and balls as I went out.

It was drizzling now, and I was damp on the head by the time I got to the hotel. And puffing, too, because no matter in what kind of condition you are, the walk up two blocks of forty-five-degree angle street sets the old pump going *potato-potato*. But it was down to a heavy *ka-boom* by the time I went into the lobby, straight to the elevator, and up to the twelfth floor.

I hesitated before knocking, wondering just how much Art had changed, and then I shrugged mentally, wondering how much I'd changed too.

The door opened immediately. Damn, no change at all, not bald, no heavier. He had always had the husky, wide shoulders of his heritage, and they were still there. He grinned widely, and grabbed my hand in his big paw.

"Phil, y'ole bastard," he said, and then pulled me into the room. He drew me close and hugged me, big as I was, and I threw my arms around him too. His body felt like steel beneath his shirt, huge hunky muscles. He had not let himself go any more than I had. Finally he released me from his crushing bearhug and stood back.

"I'll be damned," he said. "You don't look a day older than you did eight years ago."

"Nor you," I said.

"Have a drink," he said.

"Bourbon . . . rocks," I said.

He splashed some bourbon over some ice cubes and handed it to me. Then he sat down on the edge of the bed. "Tell me what you've been doin'."

I waggled my hand. "Evidently you know," I said. "More important . . . what've you been doin'?"

56

We talked for about fifteen minutes. He'd been married once and then divorced after his wife caught him in bed with a boy. He was now a well-paid vice president for an electronics firm, and lived in a town in Pennsylvania with the improbable name of Indiana. He'd discovered what he was about a year after his marriage.

"As if I didn't know all the time," I said. "But oh, no, you wouldn't ever give in. What didja think about the one time we made it together?"

"Didn't like it the next morning," he said, "but after about two weeks I found myself thinkin' about it all the time. That's when I really began to experiment . . . but I was always tellin' myself I wasn't a club member . . . just liked sex."

"Me, too, man," I said, and then reached down to slip off my shoes. They were still so unworn and new, though about a year old, that I caught the heady smell of warm new leather when I took them off. It always excited me. "Whatdyuh want to do?" I asked.

He shrugged. "Doesn't matter," he said. "Just sex. Let's see what happens."

I grinned. "If I'm agonna blow you, buddy," I said, "you've gotta wash the spit off before you screw me."

"I wouldn't argue with a pro," he grinned. "But why?"

"Don'tcha know, ole buddy? Saliva's got a helluva lot of bacteria in it, and once it gets growin' inside your asshole . . . well, watch out. You know how dangerous a human bite is. You learn a lot of these things bein' a whore."

"How long you gonna keep at this?"

I shrugged. "Not much longer," I said.

We both stepped out of our pants at the same time. His body was smooth on the upper half, and hairy from the waist down. A brute strength radiated from his well-made frame. The definition of his muscles was crisp and clear. There was no fat on him, and he must have weighed two-twenty. But when you're six-three, that's no problem.

"Damn," I said, looking admiringly at him. "With a body like that, you oughta have half the guys in Pennsylvania knockin' at your door."

"I get enough," he grinned. "But right now I want you." Naked, he sank to his knees in front of me, his big paws on my legs, hands that were so big they reached halfway around my thighs. He looked up at me. "I've wanted this for eight years," he said. "Ever since you had mine . . . and got my cherry."

I ran my fingers through his wavy brown hair. Ole Betsy had risen and was proud and straight in front of me, all a result of watching him undress. Then I cupped one hand behind his head and drew him towards my crotch.

He didn't need any urging. He opened his mouth wide and sank it down on my cock, clear to my pubic hair, nuzzling his face sidewise, back and forth, while my cockhead rubbed against the hot back wall of his throat.

He'd evidently had a lot of practice. He breathed easily and without gagging, or rather, he didn't seem to be breathing at all. And then I realized that he could hold enough air in that massive chest to keep sucking for three minutes before he needed more. I started to move my hips, gently fucking his handsome high-cheekboned face, and feeling the clamp-clamp of the membrane ring as I slid my prick back and forth through it. I could feel his throat muscles hard on my cock like a vise of velvet.

Hell, I'd always liked this cat, I realized. Not love, nosiree, but a response that even a hetero would make to the physical aura of strong animality — sexuality — that came out of all his pores. It was that curious Y quality of masculinity that attracted both men and women.

I drew away from him, my cock glistening with his saliva. "C'mon, brown-eyes," I said, grinning. "Let's get comfortable." Through the not-quite-closed slats of the Venetian blind I saw the spider web of the Bay bridge, half obscured by fog and rain, and then returned my eyes to the strong-muscled stud kneeling in front of me.

"I think I'm gonna fuck you, man," I said, and took a step toward the bathroom. "After I wash my cock off."

He laughed and grabbed my wrist with a grip like a steel vise. "Oh, no, you're not," he said. "I'm gonna fuck you. And then mebbe blow you. The customer's always right, isn't he?"

I groaned, looking at that thick long brown cock that pointed upward from his crotch, a gut-arranger for sure, its head massive and almost purple with the raging blood inside it. "You pay the hospital bill to get me stitched up?" I asked.

"You won't be split," he said. "This bohunk knows how to fuck. I've managed to get this thing into smaller assholes than yours, I betcha. Think of all those young coal miners around Wheeling that had to spend a coupla hours in Art's shack before they got hired. I screwed every damn one of 'em, farm boys and all." He grabbed his cock at its base with his fist and spread his legs apart.

"It may take me a while to get in," he said, "but you won't feel anything at all."

I reached for my pants. "Then I don't want it."

He laughed and grabbed them from me. "Still the same old smartass," he said. Then he went to the window and drew the drapes. The room was suddenly turned into a half-gloom through which he moved like a living statue, the play of muscles in the half-light making my loins surge with lust.

He opened the drawer of the night-table and pulled out a tube, getting a coupla inches of grease on his fingers. "Bend over," he said, his voice huskier than it had been.

I bent over the side of the bed, spreading my legs wide, and looked back at him through the tangled thicket of my armpit hair. All I could see of him was his left side from his belly down, and the moving column of his thick-ribbed cock as his body approached. He put a massive hand against the left cheek of my ass, pulling it sidewise, and laid the grease right on my asshole—no fumbling to find the keyhole to the celestial gate. I heard him put the rest of it on his cock—a

59

soft, hard-to-translate sound unless you've heard it a thousand times.

I was not quite prepared for the next movement he made. With one hard plunge of his forearm, he rammed his middle finger into my asshole, clear to the last knuckle.

"Hey-yi!" I said, and arched my back. It hurt, but not all that much.

He chuckled. "Just wanted to see if this's a virgin tract I'm headin' for," he said. "It don't look too stretched out," he said, "but I reckon it ain't virgin."

"Hardly," I grumbled, subsiding at the bedside again.

He evidently liked to play games with my asshole. He turned and twisted that long middle finger, thicker than some cocks I'd seen, and then, with the palm downward, he reached in and stroked my prostate. I gasped a little with the curious mixture of pain and pleasure which that massage always brought. He kept at it, digging away, stroking each side of it, first with the ball of his fingertip and then sliding the back of his fingernail down the other side. A few drops of milky prostate fluid seeped from the end of my cock and lost themselves in the rich green carpeting of the room.

Then he turned his hand palm up, and I felt him bend his finger, crooking it so that he could explore the top and bottom edges inside my sphincter. It felt wonderful, and he certainly knew what he was doing. Satisfied, seemingly, he drew his finger nearly out, but then I felt him advance his forefinger beside the middle one. This time he worked them against each other like a pair of knitting needles (but oh, what big thick ones, grandmaw!) and twiddling them a little, got the second finger started in. I groaned, and he laughed again.

"Not really a virgin tract after all," he chuckled. "At any rate, it could stand development." Both fingers were clear in, and he set up a slow twisting, rotating, that nearly drove me off the bed. My hardon bobbed wildly against the sheet, and I moved closer to the bed so that I could feel something, even

60

the sheet, to rub my cock against.

"Man," I said, panting, "you're gettin' me hot for sure."

The rich laugh again. "All you hustlers," he said. "You gotta have a little prep work to get your steam up. To get you turned on." And he pressed both fingertips hard against my prostate.

I yelped. "Oh, man," I said, "you got me turned on okay. How's about on the bed? Anyway, you didn't have to turn me on for you. I've always wanted a big hunky's cock up my ass. Yours, to be truthful."

"Oh, I'm irresistible, I am!" he chuckled. "But I ain't quite through yet."

"Man," I said desperately, "if you don't get that big hunk of meat in my ass soon, you're gonna make me pop without gettin' fucked. And you wouldn't want that now, would you?"

"Nope," he said, and with a final flick at my prostate, he withdrew his fingers and toweled them. I half-raised up. There was sweat on my face.

He looked at me. "Guess I really did get you goin'," he said. "Now, get up on the bed."

"As my royal Bohemian master commands," I said sardonically, and got a playful swat on my ass for being funny.

I climbed onto the bed. "How you want it?" I said. "On the back, doggy, or what?"

"All of 'em," he said. "Get on your back first."

I did, and spread my legs wide. He reached up across me, his cock trailing its first pearls as it slid red-hot against my chest hair, and got both pillows from the bed.

"Hoist your ass," he said. There was a tone of authority in his voice that was an echo of Larry and Greg and all the bossy ones I'd ever known. I shivered a little in anticipation.

He pulled the pillows under my ass, elevating me considerably. Then he reached for the grease again, and, opening my asshole with thumb and forefinger, stuck the tube end inside and squeezed. I felt the small jolt of coolness. His cock was rigid, and it glistened darkly in the half-light. I made a slight movement, bending my knees and starting to raise my legs.

He knocked them down. "Leave 'em flat," he said. "I told you I knew how to do it."

He hunched his massive thighs between my outspread legs, forcing them still farther apart, so that I felt split and helpless. Then he put one big paw down on each side of my cock and balls, his thumbs digging in close to my asshole, opening me still more as he pulled my asshole wider. I felt him inch closer, and then he planted his big helmeted cock-head square on target. No fumbling, no hands to find it, no nothing. That in itself told me he'd had a lot of experience. And the sensation at my asshole, the first pressure, told me something else—his cock was even bigger than it looked.

"Take it easy, will yuh?" I whispered, breathing hard. "You're big!"

"That's what all the boys tell me," he said, and I could hear the laughter in his tone. "Just relax."

I did. And then I felt the push begin—slow, inexorable. He got about half of his cockhead inside and the sphincter stopped him. Even with all his fingerwork in my ass, it hadn't opened all that much. From the feel of it, his cock was as big as all of his five fingers drawn together.

"Hm-m-m," he said. "Evidently you're more used to bein' trade than bein' fucked. That asshole's still pretty tight."

"Hell, man," I growled, looking up from my angled perspective at his huge dark form towering over me. "That cock of yours would fill the mouth of a subway."

He increased the pressure slowly, and then started small prodding, jabbing movements, circling his solid hips, and continuing the powerful push exerted by his massive thighs. I relaxed as much as I could. Now he hunched over me, and I put my hands on his tough-muscled forearms while he looked down at the progress of his cock. I gritted my teeth a little. Half of his cockhead was inside.

And then suddenly the fire-ring opened, and he slid his cock in.

I thought he would never stop. His cock went past my joy-spot, bringing an involuntary gasp from me, and then on and on until a sharp small pain told me he had hit the second sphincter. But it was a pain laced with pleasure, and I moved my legs so that I could clamp my muscles down on his cock, drawing a grunt from him.

"Hell," he said. "I guess you been fucked enough. Anybody who can work his muscles like that . . ."

With that I really bore down on him, bringing out a small yelp. "Hey!" he said. "For chrissake, don't pinch it off!"

"No fear," I said and almost started laughing, but managed to control it.

The whole length of his cock was in. It was huge, distending my sphincter, spreading the walls wide. With such a monster he could not avoid hitting my joyspot. His cock pressed heavily against it, and I moved my hips to increase my pleasure. It felt mighty good.

Then he started to fuck me, almost casually, holding his body at an angle above mine, his weight resting on his powerful, straightened arms. It was a good position, allowing me to do some muscle-work on his cock. With every forward thrust of his I tightened, and then loosened on the withdrawal.

He began to put on some more speed, twisting his hips from one side to the other and banging against the rear wall with each inward thrust, until he had me seeing a whole sky full of red stars behind my eyelids. And he was beginning to make me put out a few pearls just as his fingers in my ass had done earlier. I was groaning almost continually, not with pain but with the exquisite thrilling that is prelude to an orgasm.

My pleasure moans excited him, I guess. He drew back a few inches, taking his thick cock with him, and with an extraordinarily supple spine bent his head down towards my crotch. If I hadn't had one of the best hardons of my life, he couldn't have done it, but he lowered his face, grabbed my cock with one hand at the base and pulled up a little. I helped him with my ass upthrust as far as I could.

And he did it. He took my cock in his mouth, not much of it, about two inches I suppose, but the feel of his mouth around my cock, and the feel of his oversized prick in my ass was exquisite. And then, spine bent, he really began packing his cock into my ass—short quick strokes. I was breathing hard, released from the near-pain and pleasure of his massaging my joyspot, but now feeling the new enjoyment of his hot mouth around the end of my cock. And hearing his breathing, I exerted all my thigh and leg muscles to tighten my tunnel against him.

And was rewarded . . . His breathing grew sharp and shorter, and he started gasping as he sucked on my cock. The strokes grew quicker, and then suddenly he was twisting, writhing, his body almost in spasms, and I felt him shoot inside me, burning warm and comfortable, and (I swear it was the first time!) I felt his gyzym hit the back wall of my tunnel with force—like liquid bullets, six or seven bursts of them.

He fell on top of me, his great sweating body hard against mine, forcing his hands underneath me, while he ground his hips in a circle motion against my balls and cock and belly. His cock was still inside my asshole, although I felt it withdrawn by half. I clutched at it with my muscles once or twice, and he gave an answering throb. The smell of sweat and musk and sex, the clean hot odor of his armpits and chest, swept over me, as good almost as if I had gotten rid of my own gyzym at the same moment he did.

So he lay until his weight grew heavy on me, and then I stirred a little. "Hey, man . . ." I said.

"Yeah, I . . . know," he said. "I'm a-comin' out."

And he did. I had the odd feeling that my sphincter closed in slow motion from the great stretching it had had. Art

64

turned on his back and heaved a great bass sigh, and then he pushed one arm under my neck. "A goddamn good fuck," he said.

"You'd better believe it," I said wryly. "I feel as if I'd been stretched for a baby."

He reached up with his other hand, hooked his fingers together, and squeezed my throat. It damn near cut off my wind, and my fingers scrabbled at the steel of his muscles. He relaxed the pressure a little.

Art laughed. "Oh, I ain't through with you yet, baby," he said. "You're gonna get it again . . . in about five minutes."

"Goddlemighty, Art," I grumbled. "Right now my asshole feels like it's been reamed out with a wood rasp. Have a heart."

He chuckled. "I'll have a hardon in about a minute," he said, "if that'll do in place of a heart."

I groaned.

"I want it doggy, buster," he said and let go of my neck, pushing me over on my side. I looked in utter astonishment at his cock. It was as big and hard as it had been the first time . . . majestic, a dark tower glistening.

"Good grief," I said. "I never thought I'd see a recovery as quick as that."

He had his two fingers at the base of his cock, and rotated the head of it in a wide arc. "That's what all the boys back in Pennsylvania say," he grinned. "C'mon now," he said, and swatted me on the ass again. "Up on hands and knees like a good little ole bitch, buddy."

Groaning, I got in position, my face in the pillow which smelled fresh and clean despite everything. I felt part of his first load sliding down the inside of my thigh.

"C'mon, baby . . . be a good hustler," he said, and I laughed.

"Guess I won't need any more grease," he said. "And anyway, there's nothin' to lubricate the inside of an asshole like a good load of bohunk gyzym. My cock oughta go in real easy this time." 65

Well, of course it did. There was hardly any pain. The second time round he went at it fast, rapid fire, rabbity. His thrusts were still long and powerful. He would draw his battering ram almost out, until I felt my sphincter begin to close, and then go straight back in, full depth. In that position he swept past my prostate with each inthrust and out-pull, sending wave after wave of pleasure through me. I had a feeling that I was being pushed into paradise headfirst, and I was giving out with my pleasure moans almost continuously . . . my honest moans, not the ones I usually counterfeited.

Panting, he bent his great body over mine, almost making my knees buckle, and then I felt his two great hands clasp themselves around my waist, and, a moment later, seek and find my throbbing cock, encircling it with one great paw, grabbing it tight and working it up and down almost in time with the tempo of his fucking. The bed took up the beat, and groaned and quivered under our weight. In and out, in and out, his panting growing crescendo, his strokes even more rapid. And in my belly the warmth began, then turned to heat, and suddenly I boiled out over his hand, my cock spurting gyzym which his jacking off spread the length of my cockshaft, lubricating and cooling it at the same time. The contractions of my asshole when I came were powerful, and I thought they would never stop. And those clampings on his cock were just what he needed. He let go of my still-flowing cock, grabbed me tight around the waist, and with giant thrusts smashed against my ass, one, two, four times, and then as quickly stopped, while his gyzym poured into me for the second time in a half hour. Chest heaving, wet with sweat, he collapsed on top of me. My knees gave way and I was pushed flat on the bed, covered and enfolded by him, feeling his hot breath rapid on my neck, feeling the puddles of sweat forced out from between our bodies, to run down the sides of my hips.

"Jee-zus!" he said, in two drawn-out syllables. "That was tops, man."

His cock in my asshole was softening. I turned my head a little. "Yeah," I said, somewhat weak and weary. It was not very often you got such an enthusiastic greeting from an old school chum.

"I've thought . . . about that . . . for a long time," he said, still breathless.

"So've I," I said, "but at least I've got one thing in my memory book that you haven't."

"Yeah," he said, his fingers underneath me, twisting the hair on my chest. "The other was okay for a first time, but this's the real thing."

Our breathing was back to normal. I moved on the bed. "Time to retire?" I said, half a question.

"Yeah," he said. He began slowly to withdraw, and I could almost hear my asshole shut down for vacation when the softening cockhead came out.

"I made a mistake, though," he said dreamily, on his back. "I should have told you I'm no good for anything after I come a second time. Can't blow you or anything."

"What the hell," I said, punching him on his hard chest. "I came . . . or don't you remember? And anyway, you're the customer, and he's always right, huh?"

I had a moment of silence, thinking how I liked having his seed in me, and how I liked having been joined to him by his steel-hard rod. We are all separated from each other, except for that brief connection. Symbolically, it was a gesture I realized I'd wanted for a long time, too. His manhood overcame me; his physical power and presence made me almost limp, a kind of feminine melting, and god knows I was a man, and strong enough myself.

"Have dinner with me?" he asked, one great thigh flung heavy across my legs, one hand stroking my chest hair, rolling a nipple back and forth lightly between thumb and forefinger.

But each man is an island, despite ole John Donne. There was no sense in getting further into this thing. That was me, man. No complications. Sex and plenty of it, but I intended to shy away from all emotional involvements.

"Sorry, man," I said. "I'd sure as hell like to, but I'm goin' out to dinner tonight. Old man on Pacific Heights likes to cook for me, and I have to eat naked at his table." A lie, of course—no date tonight. But I thought it better to leave.

"Okay," he said. He didn't really want to, I guessed.

I got up and went to the bathroom to wash and then came back. He had his briefs on, and had turned on one lamp against the gathering darkness outside. He sat in an armchair, legs stretched wide apart, and the sight of that bulge was still exciting. In one hand, hanging over the chair, were some bills. Even at that distance my practiced eye picked out two twenties and a ten. "Here y'are," he said, extending them.

I took them, hating to do it, but business was business. "Thanks, man," I said. "When you come to town next time, we'll have one on the house. Free."

He shook his head. "Not if you're in the same line of work," he said. "I'm loaded."

"Lucky you," I said sardonically. "I may not be whorin' by that time. But you can be sure of one thing . . ."

"What's that?"

"Next time I'm gonna pop first," I grinned at him. "I'm really gonna cash in on that blowjob I gave you eight years ago."

He laughed. "Okay," he said. "Turn about's only fair."

"I get 'em," I said, "even if I have to wait twenty years."

And I laughed and left.

6. Oink, Oink

The next morning it was still overcast, and I found Jerry in the living room biting the knuckle of his first finger in frustration.

"Goddamn it," he said. "This fuckin' weather's never gonna let up."

"Ain't there any scenes you can shoot in the rain?"

"Ah, yeah," he said. "Lots of stuff with scenery in it, as long as it isn't *too* dark. You get the best color tones of shrubbery and trees and rocks and sand when it's overcast. But hell," he went on, "you can't do anything with bodies or closeups when they're shivering. I tried it in one film and shit! you could even see the goose bumps as they were fuckin'."

"Not the best effect," I said.

"Nope," he said. Then he turned to me. "Didja think any more about some ideas for a plot?"

"Yup," I said, and I outlined the episodes. "An' you could tie them all together," I said, "by havin' your 'hero' be gettin' a blowjob in . . . say . . . an underground parking lot, and bein' scraped to death and tryin' to come by thinking of some of his past experiences. Flashbacks, y'understand."

Jerry was silent a minute and then he looked at me. He was

69

glowing a little. "Say, that sounds okay," he said. "Could you run me up some dialogue about those stories if I lay the bread on you?"

"I hate to," I said, "but I will. But whyncha do what that bigshot eastern moviemaker does? Get all your characters stoned on grass and then just record what they say?"

Jerry made an impatient gesture with his shoulders. "Shit," he said, "none of these dudes got enough grey cells working to come up with anything more than grunts." He looked slyly at me. "Of course," he said, "with one exception . . ." and he laughed. "The star. The antihero. Yourself."

"I'm deeply touched," I said ironically. "Okay . . . I'll give it a think."

"Have it ready tomorrow?" Jerry grinned.

"You bastard," I said. "Always want it done yesterday." Then I stood up. "I'll see what can be done. Use your typewriter?"

"Sure," he said.

I stretched and started to leave. Just then the phone rang. Jerry reached out for it and answered by giving the number, the way he always did. I sat back down.

"Yeah," he said, and then paused. "Well, the escort service is pretty full right now . . . but I might be able to use you as a model . . ."

I could hear the sound of the guy's voice rattling the earpiece of the telephone, even though Jerry had it close to his ear. It was very bass and masculine-sounding.

Jerry asked his name and then said, "Who recommended you?"

Another pause. "Oh, sure . . . I remember him," he said. "Describe yourself a little."

I could still hear the voice making the tin diaphragm rumble, but I couldn't understand what was being said.

"Yeah," Jerry said. "Why don'tcha drop by about seven-thirty tonight, and we'll see if we can fit you in." Then he gave the Mason Street address and hung up. He turned to me. "Looks like we got ourselves a new stud," he said. "Down on his luck. Name of Les Jackson . . . six-one, one-eighty, black hair, and hung . . . he said."

I waggled my hand. "Hell," I said. "You've gotta see it to believe it."

"Yeah," Jerry said.

"Who recommended him?"

"Guy named John Gore," Jerry said. "Used to work for me."

The name was unfamiliar, and yet it seemed to punch one recall-key somewhere in my computer. I couldn't place it. I shook my head a little.

"Sumpin wrong?" Jerry asked.

"Don't know whether I've heard the name or not," I said. "I always seem to hang the odd names away in some closet. That 'Gore' has an association, but I can't think what it is."

"You're thinkin' of the writer."

I shook a negative at him. "Nope," I said. "Not as a last name."

"Well," Jerry said, "maybe it'll come to you."

"Yeah." I stood up again, hearing deep inside me the small flutelike voice of Dame Nature calling me to my daily rendezvous with her. "I'll be around," I said, and started for the bathroom.

When I finished there I went back to number seven. Tex-ass and Davey were out on calls—one to Berkeley and one to Sausalito. The eaves were still dripping and the day was dismal. I sat down on the bed and pulled off my boots, and picked up a copy of the gay newspaper devoted exclusively to Our Cause.

I had just thrown the newspaper on the floor when a stroke of lightning hit me right in my midbrain, followed by another directly from my subconscious, both of them tied together by the faintly overheard rumble from the earpiece while Jerry was talking with the prospective model . . . hustler. I sat straight up in bed, grabbed the newspaper, swung my legs over the side, and sock-footed it without my boots down the hall to Jerry, still sitting on the sofa.

"Hey!" I yelled.

He looked up, startled. "What gives?"

"Lissen," I said, talking so fast my words fell over each other. "This . . . John Gore . . . you got any old copies of this around?" I shook the paper at him.

"Yeah," he said.

"How far back?"

"How far you want?"

"A year, maybe eighteen months," I said.

"What's up? Why?"

"This cat named Gore got two to fourteen in Soledad," I said, "about a year ago. Trapped over at Land's End in the john. It was in the paper," I said, rattling it again. "And he ain't been released yet by any means."

"Maybe there's two John Gores," Jerry said, but he'd paled a little.

"Not much chance," I said. "And the second point's this. Your new stud's named Les Jackson . . . right?"

"That's what he said," Jerry admitted.

"One of the things about a guy's taking another name," I said, "chances are eight outa ten he uses a name with the same initials. Les Jackson . . . Larry Johnson . . . you remember that I told you about that fuckin' treacherous pig from the SFPD that nearly got me thrown in the pokey for bein' a male whore?"

"The one you told the fuzz about while he was in the Academy and then stashed some dope in the house?"

"The same one," I said. "That bass rumble on the telephone, that's what triggered me. Heard it while you were talkin' to him. Goddamnit," I swore, throwing the paper on the floor, "I wish I'd listened on the extension."

By this time Jerry was nearly grey in the face. His back jaw muscles were working as he kept biting down on his teeth. Finally he said, "You think the fuzz is out to get me?"

"I do, by God."

His knuckle went back between his teeth. "What'll we do?"

I sat down heavily. "Lemme think," I said—and did, for about two minutes.

It's odd how your mind speeds up when you're pressured. And mine did. "Evidently the fuzz didn't fall for the trap I set," I said, chewing at my own knuckle. "If this's the same person. If it is, we gotta get something on him, and I gotta stay outa the way while we're doin' it."

Then I remembered. Jerry was a mechanical genius, very skillful when it came to machinery, especially cameras. About a year ago he had developed a "soft" movie camera, one which didn't whir or click while he was photographing with it. There'd been a good reason: most of his movie "stars" were amateurs, and the very sound of the camera turning made them freeze.

"You still got your silent camera? The one that doesn't make a noise?"

Jerry nodded. "Use it all the time," he said. "Good for beginners."

"Good," I said. "And I take it you've still got that fake one-way mirror trained into Tex's room?" I hadn't sneaked a gander through it in a long time.

"Sure have," he said. "But you're the only one knows about it."

"I haven't looked through it for quite a while," I said.

"I have," Jerry said. "Matter-of-fact, I watched through it just after I got back from L.A. Saw my superstar," he grinned, "fuckin' ole Tex-ass while he was getting over his lacerations."

"Goddamn," I said. "You bastard." Then I shrugged and grinned. "There's some Peeping Tom in all of us, ain't there? How'd I do?"

Jerry grinned too. "All right," he said. "I got a stinkin' hardon just watching."

"You didn't film it?"

He shook his head. "Nope," he said, holding up three fingers of his hand in the Boy Scout oath. "Honest."

"I oughta screw the hell outa you for that," I grumbled.

"Promises," Jerry said, and then grew sober. "What's the plan?"

"Simple," I said. "If this Les Jackson really is Larry Johnson, tell him you've gotta know if he'll work out, and then put him in the room with one of the boys and make Les blow him. And photograph him while he does."

Jerry smacked his fist into his palm. "Damn," he said. "He'd be in trouble then for sure."

" 'Specially if you let him know it was all down on film," I said, still miffed that my elaborate scheme to trap the fuzz a year ago evidently hadn't worked.

Then Jerry stopped grinning. "Can't do it," he said. "It'd involve one of the guys . . . and this stud might manage to squirm out of this one, too. How's about your being the score?"

"Not a chance," I said. "He'd recognize me. But wait," I said, remembering. "I think I can get you a guy to do it."

"Who?"

I reached for the telephone book. "Name of Art Kain," I said, "if he's still in town." I found the hotel's number and dialed.

Art was still there, by gum. He answered the phone and we went through the amenities. Then I said, "Lissen, Art, there's a guy here just dyin' to blow a big bohunk like you. He's from outa town too, and he'll be down here at the whorehouse at seven tonight. Can you make it? Or do you wanta?"

Art's heavy baritone laugh rang in my ear. "Rather have you," he said. "But who's to turn down a blowjob? Sure . . . I can eat later."

"And guess what?" I said. "It's on the house. Free. Gratis."

"What's the catch?" Art asked.

"No catch. This dude's just about to become a stableboy," I said. "And we gotta try him out. Then you can report on how well he did. All the guys except me are busy tonight, or we'd use one of them," I added.

"Why not lemme have you, ole buddy?"

I used a sorrowful tone. "After the way you mistreated and abused me yesterday, I'm outa service for a few days. Besides, we want to get a nonprofessional opinion on a new boy."

"I'm flattered," Art said. I could almost see his smirk.

"No kiddin'. Can we count on you?"

"Sure . . . See you at seven."

I hung up and looked at Jerry. "Get it ready," I said. "Set it all up. Art Kain'll be here at seven."

Jerry looked perturbed. "But what if Les Jackson ain't your fuzz?"

I shrugged and turned my palms up in a continental gesture. "Let whoever it is blow Art Kain anyway," I said. "Or . . ." and I grinned, "you can sacrifice yourself on the altar of Venus. You'll like him, even if he is old enough to have to shave every day."

7. A Foxy Scheme

It was a sort of nervous supper we had that evening about five-thirty. There were only four of us there—Teddy, Davey, Jerry, and myself. The others were out. And we were tense. Jerry had to let them all in on what was happening, and most of us realized how dangerous it was, if this were really Larry Johnson.

"Davey," Jerry said. "You and Teddy'll be in the room where the camera's set up. And Phil . . . you be in the bathroom so's you can get a good look-and-listen. I'll take him into the living room and talk for a coupla minutes, asking the usual questions—"

I shook my head. "Not the usual ones," I said. "More discreet. Make out that you've got an up-and-up modeling service. Or escort bureau. For both men and women."

"Good idea," Jerry said. "Then I'll take him into the back bedroom and ask him to strip. Just in the interests of good business, of course."

"Of course," I said cynically. "Get him to leave his clothes there. Then you can check his ID in his wallet. Or see if he carries a big flashy star . . ."

Jerry shuddered. "I'll be so fuckin' nervous . . ." he began.

"Ah, hell . . . you've been in tighter scrapes than this," I said. "And anyway, it may not be Johnson at all."

"I looked up that old article in the newspaper," Teddy said. "The guy was named John Gore, all right. The fuzz could've got a lot of information from him." He waved a copy of the paper in the air. Then in his irrepressible way, he giggled. "Jerry," he said, "can I move in that room next to Tex's? I gotta lot of catchin' up to do on my sex education."

Jerry swatted him on the ass, but the remark relaxed us somewhat. Then he said to me, "I sure as hell hope your Art Kain gets here on time."

"You're not plannin' to tell him what's up, are you? He'd leave in a minute," I said.

"No," Jerry said. "I'd like to have him undressed and ready in Tex's room before your guy gets here."

"What are you gonna do for light?" I asked.

"There's enough, what with daylight saving. And," he said, "on second thought, I'll take down the window shade in Tex's room and jimmy the switch to the overhead light. Besides, I've got a real fast film in the camera."

I nodded. "Where did you say Teddy's gonna be?"

"In the camera room with Davey. Davey can handle the sound and Teddy and I'll do the film."

"And I'll come in just to watch," I grinned. "I like bein' a voyeur. Besides, Art Kain still turns me on . . . and much as I hate to admit it, so does that Johnson bastard. If it's really Larry."

Jerry looked at his watch. "Let's get crackin'," he said. He went to the kitchen and got the stepladder. "For the window shade," he said. Tex's window looked out on a blank sunlit wooden wall; there was no possibility of anyone seeing in.

"Davey," Jerry said. "Can you fix the switch? Disconnect one wire and insulate it, so it won't turn off?"

"Sure," Davey said, tossing his long blond hair. "If you'll tell me where the circuit breaker is."

"In the laundry room," Jerry said. I helped Jerry with the stepladder. Davey disappeared and in a moment the lights went off in Tex's room. Then Davey was back in the doorway with a screwdriver and went to work on the switch. Jerry climbed the ladder and unhooked the window shade, and handed it to me. Then he climbed down. Davey vanished again and in a few minutes the light came on. I worked the switch. It didn't function; the ceiling light stayed on.

"I just happened to think of something else," I said. "Probably both of them will want to take a leak before they begin . . . and I'll be in the bathroom."

Jerry said, "You and I can meet your Art Kain and talk to him in the living room and later I'll leave. Then you can see if he wants to piss before you take him to Tex's room. And then when I've got Les—or Larry—in the back bedroom askin' him to strip, you can get out of the john and come into the camera room. If you want to watch, that is."

"What if he tries to bust you before anything happens?" I asked.

Teddy spoke up. "I don't think he will," he said. "He probably wants to work himself in good with the whole setup and then get everybody, not just Jerry. But if he's really gone undercover, he won't have a badge or ID . . . nothin' on him at all."

"Teddy's probably right," I said.

"And anyway," Jerry said, "bust me on what ground? Escort services are legal, and so is modeling."

"Oh sure," I said wryly. "Like Turkish baths and massage parlors. Nothing really ever happens, especially in the steam rooms."

"Well, I'm certainly not going to say anything indiscreet," Jerry said. And then he had another idea. "I'll have the tape recorder on in the living room and the back bedroom too."

"Good idea," I said.

By the time we finished our busywork, it was nearly seven o'clock. None of us seemed very nervous now, although I could tell Jerry was. I sat down in the back living room for a cigarette and found that my hands were trembling faintly. It was really like a game, but a rather deadly one. In some ways I hoped it would be Larry; in others, I wished he'd be a stranger.

The old grandfather clock in the hallway had just finished striking seven when the doorbell rang. "That'll be Art," I said.

Jerry said, "Davey, you and Teddy get into the camera room and keep quiet. I'll be there as soon as I meet Kain."

"Can't I meet him too?" Teddy asked.

"With any luck you'll see all of him soon enough. In action," Jerry said, a smile briefly twitching at his lips. And then to me: "You answer the door, huh?"

I unfolded and went down the railroad corridor to the front door. It was Art, all right, a big friendly grin showing his good white teeth, and looking even larger in his clothes than out of them. A flash at the suit and topcoat gave me a conservative estimate of about five hundred bucks. In the late sunlight his face was healthy and tan, and his wide forehead and dark brown wavy hair looked mighty good to me.

"Hiya!" he said, grinning widely. "This is sure a surprise." He grabbed my hand in his big paw, nearly enfolding it.

"C'mon in, man," I said, and shut the door behind him. "This way," and I went before him down the corridor.

Jerry was pretending to be reading. He looked up when he came in, his face registering honest shock at Art's hugeness. He stood up. Art really towered over Jerry's five-foot-nine.

"Art Kain . . . Jerry Baldwin," I said.

Now it was Jerry's hand that was hidden in Art's. I saw the fine dark hair that thickly covered the back of Art's paw, the big raised veins that mapped its surface, as Art tightened his grip on Jerry, making him wince a little.

"Damn," Jerry said. "You're quite a hunk of man. Welcome to our club."

"Thanks," Art said, looking around. "Nice pad you got here."

In the comparatively small living room, Art seemed almost

out of place. He dominated it like a colossus, an Atlas shouldering the world on his back. Big as he was, he moved with a catlike grace that made me envious. Through the well-cut handsome suit I could reconstruct the massive perfection of his body, see the curve of his deltoids cutting sharply into the swelling of his triceps, and the wide smooth rounding of the plateau of his huge chest, the nipples set low and pointing downward, surrounded with almost brown-black areolas and a sprinkling of a few short dark hairs.

His heavy maleness assaulted all the senses, smothered or altered them so that you thought at first you smelled a musky sexual odor, or saw the discus throwers in the stadiums of ancient Greece.

God—he was Man! the combination of all my sexual heroes from Tarzan onward, the epitome of domination, commanding, overpowering, leaving me feeling almost as weak as a Victorian maiden approaching the wedding bed.

I glanced at Jerry and saw that the aura of Art Kain had reached him, too. He seemed almost paralyzed, and wet his lips two or three times. Finally, he was able to speak.

"Couldn't get you to leave your job and come live in our stable for a year, could I?" he asked. "You'd knock the whole town over. You'd be our superstud . . ." and then with a half-apologetic look in my direction, "except for Phil here."

I waggled my hand. "I know when I'm licked," I grinned. "Only trouble is . . . Art might never get outa the house on a call. He'd be so busy servicin' all the cats that live here, there wouldn't be time."

"Well," Jerry said, with what was obviously the greatest reluctance to leave, "I've got some things to do. Phil will lay the details on you, and I'll see you later . . ." He started to leave, and you could almost see the heavy chain on his ankle that locked him to Art's presence.

Art laughed in his rich baritone. "See you," he said.

". . . after it's over," Jerry said, backing out of the room.

"Okay," Art said. When Jerry had gone, Art grinned at

me. "I may be a hick from West Virginia," he said, "but I think that's the guy who really wants me."

"Don't we all," I said.

In an old-buddy-fraternity gesture, Art threw an arm around my shoulders. "How's about makin' it a three-way?" he asked. "Ain't had one of those in a coon's age."

I laughed, and liked the weight of his arm on me. "I'd like it too," I said, "but this is a tryout for the new stud."

"Makin' me a guinea pig, huh?" he said, tightening his arm around my neck.

I laughed again and ducked away—not that I wanted to, but . . . "Lissen," I said. "The idea's for you to go into one of the rooms and undress and be all ready for this guy when he comes in. He'll be naked, too . . . he'll probably be nervous as all hell. But if I know you, that won't last long," I said. "He'll be after that cock of yours as soon as he sees it."

"What's he gonna do?" Art asked.

"Not up to him," I said. "You're callin' the shots. You make him do what you want . . . blow you, or you screw him. Then you can tell us later what happened, and how well he did it."

"Okay," Art grinned. "I like that."

I looked at my watch. "You wanta piss first, before I take you to the room? He's due here in twenty minutes."

"I'll take a leak," Art said, starting to remove his jacket. "Or should I just undress in the room?"

"The room," I said. "I'll show you where the can is." Art suddenly grabbed me by the shoulder with one hand, whirled me around, and with the other gripped my basket. "This's what I really want," he said.

I pried his fingers loose, laughing. "Next time," I said. "C'mon . . . I'll hold it for you."

We went into the bathroom. "Unzip it," he said. "Take my cock out."

I did, trembling a little, pulling the top elastic rim of his shorts down and getting a big handful of his cock. He sighed. "The balls, too," he said.

81

It all filled my hand as it had yesterday. I could feel ole Betsy unlimbering a bend or two, swelling in my own crotch. Art was half-hard.

"C'mon," I said. "Piss." I held its red head aimed downward. He was not circumcised, but the tensing of his growing hardon had pulled the foreskin nearly back to the flange of the corona. I held it steady and finally he started — a heavy powerful stream that I guided right into the middle of the pool.

When he finished, he was almost limp again. I let go of his cock, and watched him tuck everything back inside. Then he said, "Let's go."

I led him into Tex's room, noting that Jerry had put clean sheets on the bed and neatly folded the blankets on a chair. The window was down to shut out the street noise and the ceiling light was on. A flood of golden sunlight came into the room. A quick glance showed me the microphone carefully taped in position at the back edge of the night-table. I looked toward the fake mirror, knowing the camera was trained on the bed, but I saw no shadow or lights.

"Make yourself at home," I grinned.

"If I do," Art said, beginning to strip, "I won't be any good for your stud. An' who wants to jack off when he's got a blowjob or a good fuck comin'?"

I laughed. "That wasn't exactly what I meant by 'make yourself at home.'"

Art looked around. "How about the light? Seems pretty damned bright in here."

"Wanta see what you're doin', don'tcha? Like the French. Take it easy, and I'll see you later." I closed the door, heading for the camera room. There'd be plenty of time to get into the bathroom after the doorbell rang.

The camera room was in total darkness — had to be, so no one could see in through the phony mirror. I saw the small patch of light when I opened the door, with three black silhouettes of heads leaning into it, almost entirely blocking the rectangle. I heard the almost inaudible running of the camera in the silence of the room. Someone turned to me. I could just make out that it was Jerry.

"Damn," he whispered. "That's the most man I ever saw."

"Pretty sexy, huh?" I whispered back. "You gonna get a good picture?"

"Dandy," Jerry said. "It'll be a little soft, but not blurry. The zoom'll get us fine closeups too. Come watch." He giggled quietly in the gloom. "We all got hardons already."

They made a place for me, and through the mirror I saw that Art already had his jacket and shirt off. His superb torso gleamed darkly in the yellow light. He sat down on the bed and took off his shoes and socks, slowly, deliberately. His feet were high-arched and beautiful. Then he stood up and unbuckled his belt and the top fastenings, and slid his trousers slowly down his magnificent legs, more swarthy and sexy than I'd remembered them from yesterday in the near gloom. That left him only in his briefs, bulging forward from his recent hardon in the john. Fingers at each hip, he pushed them slowly down.

Stripped, he sighed (you could hear him through the monitor microphone) and sat down on the bed naked for a moment. Then he got up, fumbled in his shirt pocket, and got a cigarette. He lighted it and lay down on the bed, one arm behind his head.

"Y'know," Jerry whispered. "Even if this new guy doesn't turn out to be your Larry, I'm gonna film it anyway. You don't often see a . . . specimen like him."

"Good show," I said, my mouth dry from looking.

We watched Art feel with his other hand around his cock, sliding it down beside his egg-sized balls, and then taking the weapon in hand. It lay nearly bent double over his fingers. He slowly gripped his cock and squeezed it a coupla times, then he reached over to put the ash in an ashtray. At that moment, the doorbell rang again.

"Damn," Jerry swore softly. "I hate to leave."

"Me too," I said. We both slipped out the door into the purposely darkened hallway, Jerry heading right, and I to the left for the bathroom. I got inside and closed the door.

And then I heard, "Jerry? I'm Les Jackson."

Hell, there was no mistaking that bass voice! It cut through walls and plaster, crisp, clean, the voice that reminded me of the sunken caves of Poseidon—not rumbling or reverberating, but keyed so strong and low that it sent the old familiar shivers down the steps of my spine. It was Larry for sure.

"Come in," Jerry said. His voice was hard to hear, not at all penetrant. "C'mon back to the living room. We'll talk a minute."

Ear to the door crack, I heard them. "Sit down there," Jerry said. The chair we'd planned for Larry faced three-quarters away from the bathroom door, so that he could not see me out of the corner of his eye.

Sonofabitch—it *was* Larry! No mistaking that hair (a little longer now than a crewcut) . . . no mustache, just the heavy blueish beardmark along his jawline. Hair color, body size, width of shoulders and chest, the tight trousers over the muscles in his long legs . . . all identical.

"Y'understand," Jerry was saying. "This is a legit escort service and modeling agency. No hankypanky at all . . . unless it's on your own time. You gotta arrange any private things all by yourself, if you want to. You get propositioned— that's none of my business. But we gotta give you a tryout to see if you can handle things with both men and women. We can't have some hung-up guy on the staff who won't do one thing or the other. So we gotta see how you perform. You ready for a session?"

Larry cleared his throat, a little nervously, I thought. "Ah . . . well . . ." he said. "I ain't so sure. I just got blowed a coupla hours ago."

"Shit, man," Jerry said. "That's the whole point of your comin' over tonight, wasn't it? To have a tryout. See if you'd

84

be any good . . . that is, if you want regular work."

"I s-sure do," Larry said, and he grinned that catchy smile I never could resist. "But I'm not sure I'd . . . do my best . . ."

"Well . . ." Jerry said, a little colder now. "If that's the way you feel about it, maybe we'd better forget it. But anyone your age oughta be able to pop three, four times a day . . ."

"Ah . . ." Larry said. He sensed he was trapped. "Well, I guess I can. What is it tonight . . . man or woman?"

"Man," Jerry said. "But let's get it straight. You don't have to go through with this if you don't want to work for me. It's your own decision . . . free will and all that crap. The guy in the bedroom's an old friend from outa town. No danger. And he knows you're just beginnin' . . ."

"Hell!" Larry said. "I ain't no amateur."

Not on your life, old boy, I thought. My feelings were all mixed up inside. I hated the bastard—and yet I remembered the wonderful way he'd treated me during those months we'd lived together while he was training to be a fuzz. Despite his treachery, the sight of him created a sexual remembrance of things past. I felt his cock in my ass, his toes in my mouth, and his cock there, too. I even sensed my cock in his ass, the night I'd fucked him, and the excitement was overwhelming. Then I hardened the old heart and remembered the way he'd tried to turn me in to the cops as a male whore.

"Before anything," Jerry was saying, "we gotta go to the bedroom and you'll have to strip, so's I can see what you've got and what to recommend to whoever wants you."

"Sure thing," Larry said. "Right now?"

"Yeah," Jerry said. "Don't worry . . . I won't touch you."

"It might cost even you if you did," Larry said. I could see him grinning. Well, that was a double-edged remark . . .

They passed out of my line of sight and I softly opened the door, turning right towards the camera room and going in quietly. There were only two heads at the window this time.

I looked. Still flooded with the darkening gold of the sun, Art lay on his back, cigarette extinguished, lazily moving his hand up and down on his cock, which stood up stony and straight as an obelisk from the middle of his body. His eyes were closed, and a contented smile curved the corners of his lips. I wondered what Olympian deity or satyr or young boy or—well, just what—was projecting itself on the screen of his fantasy. Just then Jerry came back into the camera room . . .

. . . and immediately thereafter, we all saw the door to Art's room open. Larry came in, head and shoulders first. Then he turned and quietly latched the door and threw the inner bolt. He was naked. I almost panicked at the sight of his back—the broad shoulders and narrow waist of which I knew every inch; the compact ass tightly compressed over the crease I knew so well, the gateway to my paradise that I had finger-traced so often. He faced Art, who had heard him and opened his eyes.

Larry was distinctly nervous. "H-Hi," he said.

"Hello, man," Art said from the bed. He had two fingers at the base of his cock and was slowly waving it from side to side.

Trust old Art to put you at ease. He let go of his cock and raised up on one elbow in bed, crossing his ankles. "Climb in," he said, grinning infectiously.

"Wh-What do you want to do?" Larry asked, moistening his lips a little.

Art lay back and clasped his hands behind his head. "Blow me," he said. It was neither a command or a question—just an answer to Larry's question.

I suppose not every member of the SFPD has to blow someone in order to trap him, but if a promotion lay ahead for a major bust such as this one might turn out to be, it would be worth it.

And yet at the same time, through the mirror, I was seeing proof that Larry really was a cop. He was hesitant at first, almost reluctant—well, that's what a year of no-suckee would do for you, if you were really more homo than bi. He got on his knees between Art's wide-stretched legs on the bed, took hold of his cock with his hand, and lowered his head almost as if he were praying. But his fingers clamped tight on Art's cock; you could see the white of his knuckles. "Closeup of that hand, if the white'll show," I whispered to Jerry, and he zoomed in. "Shows how much he wants it. Or somethin'."

And then suddenly that well-made body of Larry's was triggered. It seemed to go wild. He was all over Art, sucking his nipples, flat-tonguing his belly, running his mouth and tongue down Art's legs—which began to quiver—and then burying his face in Art's crotch alongside his balls, finally taking them one at a time between those deep-carved lips and hollowing his cheeks as he sucked them.

You could tell that Art was astonished at the wildness. He bent his neck upward, his eyes wide, as he watched the sexual tornado that Larry had suddenly become. The cop was all over him in a series of lithe panther movements, head turning from side to side, arms and legs quivering, hands seeking and searching, and with lips still open nibbling the underside of Art's cock, small movements, until he reached the underhead. With a turn of his face, almost as if despairing, he opened his mouth as far as he could, a pink-red gulf lined with white, and in one sudden convulsive movement, took all of Art's cock inside, burying his head against the dark crisp curls of his crotch hair. He must have missed all that in the past year.

Art's body arched upward as if someone had stung him on the ass with a cattle prod. The lunge must have hurt Larry's back throat pretty bad; he gagged—but he didn't let go.

"Oh, damn, man!" Art gasped. "That's the best!" His voice came thinly through the monitor on the recorder, but I knew it was being picked up full blast on the tape.

I saw Jerry nudge Teddyboy in the ribs, and saw him grin in the reflected light. But at the same time I saw something else. Teddy had quietly opened Davey's fly, and his hand

87

had vanished beyond the wrist into the fabric cavern of Davey's crotch. And then I saw Davey's hips moving ever so slightly back and forth. As for myself, even old Betsy was uncomfortably restricted down my own leg. *Ah, well,* I thought, *all the world loves a lover* . . . That left only Jerry for me, and somehow that evening—watching two favorite studs of mine on the bed—I guess I would have preferred beating it, while thinking of them both together. I remembered that ole Freud in the last years of his life waggled his beard and said sadly, "The more I see of two people having sexual contact, the more I am convinced there are four persons together in the same bed . . ."

Then I saw Art suddenly turn over and push Larry flat on his back. Art slid up the length of Supercop's body until his crotch was directly over Larry's mouth. Then Art reached down with his hand and separated Larry's lips with his fingers, one arm straightened and holding the magnificent machine of his dusky body up at an angle. He tapped his fingernail against the barrier of Larry's teeth.

"Open up, now," Art said. There was enough threat in the inflection to indicate what might happen if Larry kept his mouth closed.

But, like a good little boy, Larry opened. Art's wiry pubic hair came close to Larry's mouth, shadowing his lips.

"My balls again, cocksucker," Art said, and Larry obediently took them, sucking one at a time into his mouth and then releasing it. He looked up at Art with a sort of beseeching glance, which I understood, but doubted if the other watchers did.

Then Art, with his fingers around the head of his cock, slipped it into the cop's mouth, returning that hand to the bed to hold himself at an angle. And very slowly, he let his weight carry him downward. His cock gradually entered Larry's mouth, slow inch by slow inch, until Larry's whole face was obscured by the dark thicket of Art's crotch hair, and I knew that the entire length of his big cock was sunk into that deep throat.

"Ah-h-h!" Art said, in pure pleasure.

Larry said nothing—how could he? He was the conquered, and Art knew it. He withdrew his cock slowly, glistening with saliva, to give Larry a chance to get some air into his lungs. Then, as if he were doing pushups, Art started in again, sinking clear down with each thrust. I could imagine the punishment of Larry's throat, and the tickling annoyance of the pubic hair against his face and lips.

I looked down the length of Art's superb body, watching the muscles in his strong arms working, looking at the lean hard plane of his belly retreating, coming close to the face beneath him, and then retreating again. Art was using him as a straight guy would use a whore—fucking his mouth.

Then Art withdrew and paused. His voice came clearly through the monitor. "You know what?" he growled. "I'm gonna fuck the shit outa you."

And Larry's voice, saying, "Aw, man, I don't go for that much. And besides, you're so damned big."

"However," Art said huskily. "At least your asshole doesn't have teeth in it. It won't bite me." Then he grabbed Larry with both hands under the jawbone, pulled him half to a sitting position, swung off him, and pushed Larry to the edge of the bed. I smiled secretly at the lack of an authoritarian reaction, because Larry did not draw back.

"But—" he began.

"But what?"

Larry looked down. "Will you wash the spit offa your cock before you fuck me?"

I almost snorted with laughter, and Jerry looked around warningly. That was a bit of know-how that the traitor had picked up while living with me, and I guess it had stayed with him. Art got up and rubbed some soap and water over his flaming cock, casually drying it.

"Where d'they keep the grease in this whorehouse?" he asked.

Larry shook his head. "Nightstand, I reckon," he said, his bass voice really rolling through the monitor this time.

Art reached into the nightstand and found the pound jar that was in every room. He smeared some lightly along the length of his thick-ribbed cock, and then leaned over to push a gob of it in the crack of Larry's ass, massaging it well in with his fingers. From the way Larry's head arched back, and his clearly heard gasp, we all knew that Art's finger had gone inside as well.

"Okay, cunt," Art growled. He got on the bed on his knees, but Larry remained motionless.

"C'mon, baby," he said threateningly, but at the same time he swung himself off the bed. He'd evidently changed his mind about something. He pulled the two pillows from the bed and plopped them on the floor, and then grabbed a startled Larry's legs and pulled him, so that Larry's ass stuck out just a little over the edge of the bed.

"I guess I'll stand up and fuck you, cunt," Art said. "You can just pretend you're on the kitchen table along with all the other cans . . . of goodies."

The faintest ghost of a smile (the first I'd seen on him that day) flickered across Larry's lips, and he calmed down a little, judging from the expression on his face.

Art advanced toward him and got in between his legs. Both their bodies were in profile to the camera, and I could even see the rosy-brown tint of Larry's puckered asshole as Art raised Larry's legs up to rest on his shoulders. Art stood beside the bed, legs braced apart. His feet were on the pillows, and I wondered why. Then all of a sudden I thought I knew, remembering a bronzed and sexual workman I'd known in Rome once . . .

Art grabbed Larry's legs and swung them high in the air. It was only natural for Larry to cross his ankles and lock them behind Art's neck.

"Here we go, man," Art rumbled. "You'd better relax."

And then I saw another thing, another small revelation.

Anyone who's being unwillingly fucked is not cooperative; he keeps himself passive. But there was a small wiggle to Larry's upturned ass as he adjusted himself in position, and then I saw one of his hands creep down towards his own crotch and pass beside his balls, to guide Art's dark and swollen cockhead to its proper place. His gasp as Art pushed, after Larry had placed it dead center, came sharply through the recorder. Art swatted him on the ribcage. "Relax, I told you, damnit!" he said, almost angrily.

In the darkness of the camera room I looked cautiously aside; Teddy had Davey's cock out by now and was brazenly jacking him off. Jerry didn't even see it; he was too busy adjusting his own crotch and working the zoom on the camera, and doing the slow angling of the lens.

What the fuck, I thought, and opened my own fly, feeling the friendly comfort of my hand around my cock. I was stimulated as all hell.

From then on we were treated to one of the most exciting humpings I had ever seen — like two dinosaurs making love. I was hardly aware of my own breathing. My armpits and crotch felt as if tongues of fire had flamed in them; my forehead and hands were wet with sweat, and the speed of my jacking-off increased.

Art crouched over Larry. I could see his thick brown cock swaying between his legs as he gently moved from side to side, drawing closer to Larry's exposed asshole until the head disappeared from view into the cleft of Larry's ass. His hero's body swung right, then left, and the grimace of pain told us that Art was entering slowly and unrelentingly. Those sidewise swings would open any ring, and they must have opened Supercop's, because in less than thirty seconds Art's cock had entirely vanished from view, and the thick bush of his pubic hair was closely pressed against Larry's widely opened ass.

Art clasped his arms around Larry's thighs from underneath, and began to back away from the bed, grinning widely and pulling Larry with him.

And then suddenly—plop! Art pulled him off the bed so that his head and shoulders struck the pillows, his legs straight up in the air. Art's cock was still in his asshole.

"Hey . . . what the fuck!" Larry yelled, struggling, his elbows bent and his hands against the cheeks of his ass to support himself.

I nudged Jerry. "That's the ole Roman upside-down fuck," I said.

Jerry grinned in the gloom. "Obviously," he said.

The mechanics of the position made Larry unhook his ankles from their clamped position around Art's muscular neck, and as Larry unwound himself, Art ducked his head so that his body was between Supercop's legs, one foot at his back, the other right at his mouth. I was pleased to see Art raise that foot a bit, whether intentionally or accidentally, so that it rested on the heel, and plant the toes directly over Larry's mouth.

Larry must have been damned uncomfortable. He recrossed his ankles and locked them over Art's shoulder. But that fucking handsome stud double-crosser was game to the end. He used his locked legs to start drawing himself upward to meet Art's continuing downward thrusts, so that they jarred together in rhythm, Art's cock sinking deeply into Larry's ass. It takes two real he-men to fuck in that position.

Through the monitor we could hear them panting from their exertions; through the window we could even see the sweat rolling down their bodies. Larry must really have been suffering because I knew that position—the neck and shoulders were constricted in sharp pain from such a placing.

Suddenly Art let out a wild cry of "Oh, Jee-zus!" and froze in a wide-stanced pose, while his belly heaved and contracted from washboard to ripple, and at the same moment—without being touched—Larry's hard down-pointing cock exploded, scattering and sprinkling gyzym all over his chest, chin, face, and even into his own mouth, which opened with his orgasm. He grimaced, and then— wonder of wonders!—subsided, licking his tongue around his under and upper lips, seeking and taking up the pearly drops of his own come.

Jerry turned to me and made a circle with his thumb and forefinger, grinning, and then grinned even more when he saw me jacking off. He looked sidewise and saw the blur of motion as Teddy masturbated Davey. "Go on, kid, if you want to," he whispered to Teddy. "I already shot in my pants."

In the half-light—much darker now, but still lighted through the see-through mirror from the light in the other room—I saw Teddy sink to his knees and start to suck Davey's cock, while Davey threw his head back, and . . .

But I never saw what happened. My own cock burst, the skin seeming to rip apart with the force of my ejaculation, and spurt after spurt gushed forth, all over the back of Jerry's pants, the camera, tripod, everything. Jerry felt it. He turned, but instead of being pissed off, he was silently laughing.

"Et tu, Brute," he said. "Wonder why sex is so much more exciting if you're a voyeur."

"Tell me that," I said, "and I'll tell you how many flies are in every bar in San Francisco." I stuffed my cock back in my pants where it went on quietly dribbling. We were certainly a wet and bedraggled bunch in that camera room.

Jerry laughed softly and then sobered. Davey and Teddy were tucking things away. "Well," Jerry said, "whatever happens now, we've got the goods on your agent provocateur. Your goddamned hypocritical fuzz."

"Since I helped," I said, "how's about makin' a print of that for me?"

Jerry looked doubtful. Anything that cost him money and brought no return was comparatively no-no.

"C'mon, man," I said. "Hadn't been for me, you might've taken that cop in and trusted him completely . . . until he busted you."

Jerry nodded. "You're right," he said. "I'll have one made for you."

Heart singing, little bluebell plans for blackmail dancing happily in my head, I buttoned my fly and headed for Pete's room across the hall.

8. A Confrontation

I was almost out the door of the camera room when a soft "Ps-s-t!" from Jerry stopped me. He beckoned me back.

"Hey," he said, pointing. I looked through the mirror. Art Kain was already half-dressed, very businesslike about the whole thing, while my young traitorous pig-stud was sitting disconsolately on the edge of the bed, his cock still hard and swollen and sticking up from the black bush between his legs. More proof how gay he was.

"Listen," Jerry said rapidly and softly. "I'll have to go out and talk to Art Kain and ask him how he liked it and all that sort of crap. But somehow I think we'd better not let Larry get back to the Hall of Justice with his report . . . I mean, we gotta let him know right now that he's been filmed. Whatdyuh think?"

I saw the danger of letting him get away with a preliminary account, even though I knew it would be revised and doctored to make himself blameless. "Damn," I said, and scratched my head. "You're right."

"You feel up to a confrontation with Larry right now?" Jerry asked. "I somehow think you're the one to tell him."

It was about the last thing in the world that I wanted, but I realized that Jerry was right. "Okay," I said. "Only you'd better get Art out of here first. It's likely to get kinda loud."

Jerry nodded. "As soon as Kain comes out, I'll take him back to the living room and you can come out and say good-bye, and meanwhile I'll send Teddy in to tell Larry to wait a few minutes."

"His clothes are back in the other bedroom."

Jerry shrugged. "So . . . he'll wait naked. And Teddy," he said, turning. "You be goddamned sure you call him Les, not Larry. Got it?"

Teddy nodded.

". . . and take your arm off Davey's waist," Jerry said savagely. "Or I'll put you on bread and water for a week."

Teddy giggled. "I might get too fat that way," he said, but he withdrew his arm.

Jerry and I slipped out, and were just passing Tex's room when Art opened his door. I stepped quickly beyond range, and Art closed the door behind him. Jerry motioned us into the living room, and I shut the door after us.

"Well," said Jerry, "how'd it go?"

"Wild, man," Art grinned. "That stud acted like he hadn't had sex for a year. Seemed a little nervous at first, but man, he sure got over that fast. He oughta be a good addition to your house."

"Satisfactory, then, huh?" Jerry asked, grinning.

"More than," Art said. "And I'd like to stay around and rap with you guys, but I got a business date at eight-thirty for dinner, and I've gotta get back." He stuck out his huge hand and Jerry shook it. Then Art turned to me. "And as for you, y'ole bastard, I'll be back in town in about six months and see you then."

I shook his hand. "Yeah," I said, grinning. "Account I'm gonna collect on a small debt you've owed me for eight years . . ."

"Don't worry . . . I'll pay up," Art said, flashing that heart-stopping smile.

With another ear leaning toward the hallway, I heard the

door of Tex's room open, heard Teddy deliver the message, and then close the door again. I relaxed a little; the timing was too goddamned close around here.

Then Art was gone. Somehow the lights all seemed to dim with his departure, the street noises grew louder, and I heard the flames burning high under the hot-water heater. With Art in the room, all those other things were blanketed; the force he put out was as close to human magnetism as anything I'd ever experienced. I drew a deep breath.

Jerry turned to me. "Well, are you ready?"

"Got a baseball bat? Meat cleaver? Battleaxe? . . . You may need them after this session is over. Are you gonna film it?"

"Sure," Jerry said. "We'll get all on him we can. Whyncha make him blow you and then you can take sloppy seconds on him too. He must still be hot."

I took another deep breath. "Shit," I said. "I hate this like hell."

Jerry patted my arm in an almost motherly fashion. I jerked aside in irritation. "Yeah, I know," he said, "but think what he tried to do to you."

"The trouble is," I said, "I still like the sonofabitch. He turns me on. Don'tcha think he's a good-lookin' stud?"

"Handsome as the wine-dark sea," Jerry smiled.

Teddy came into the room. "Hey," he said softly. "You'd better get in there in a hurry. He was beatin' his meat when I opened the door."

So this was it. As I took the few steps to Tex's room, I remembered a lot of things—picking Larry out of the gutter in Berkeley when he was spaced-out on acid, the smell of the dusty rug and the feel of his foot against my neck as he made me lick up my own gyzym spilled on the floor, the night I'd screwed him when he was high on grass, the sound of his voice rattling the windows of the small house in Berkeley, and the agony of finding the police-report blanks. But mostly I recalled—and ole Betsy showed that she remembered, too, by her stirring—the times he'd fucked me, the feel of his big cock plugging my ass and the dancing over my joyspot that he'd learned to do so well, the sensation of his throat muscles tight-pressing against my cock, forming the vibrating hot canal that received all I had to give him . . .

I put my hand on the doorknob, hesitated a moment, then turned it and went in, almost backing in, my face turned away from the bed so that he could not yet see anything except the leather jacket. I closed the door and turned around slowly, feeling the doorknob press into my butt as I leaned against it, folded my arms, and crossed one boot over the other.

"Well, well," I said, "look who's here."

It was difficult to analyze his expression. At first I thought I saw a glint of terror—or maybe only surprise—but it was followed quickly by recognition, and then the black wings of his eyebrows drew down together into a scowl. He had let go of his cock—the old familiar thick-corded circumcised cock with the head that always reminded me of a small German helmet.

"You!" he said viciously.

I maintained a calm I did not exactly feel. "Yup," I said. "Me."

He half-rose from the bed in a sort of tiger crouch, as if he were ready to spring. "You motherfucker!" he said, and again I almost heard the windows rattle, the same way they used to do when we lived together. "You . . . know what you did, stashing that . . . goddamned dope in your fuckin' h-house in Berkeley?" He was so mad he half-choked on the words.

"Kept you out of the SFPD, I hope," I said.

That's one thing about anger. If you're furious, you're likely to blurt out. And he did. "N-Not q-quite, you sonofa-bitch," he said low and hard, and swallowed noisily.

"Oh," I said. "So you did get in after all. And now you're here to bust us."

He looked as if he wished he'd bitten his tongue off.

"G-Goddamn it . . . yes," he said. He looked madder'n hell.

"Well," I said, "you sure blew this assignment. What was it . . . your first? And," I said, still holding on, "you blew it more than you think. This time something else has happened. You've been on camera. We've got a full four hundred feet of you blowing that bohunk and gettin' fucked by him."

He looked wildly around the room. "H-How?" he stuttered. "Wh-where?"

"Never mind," I said. "You'd never find it. And the film's already on the way to Jerry's processor. The point is, I just thought you'd like to know all that before you write up your report."

I guess the shock was pretty bad. His mouth fell open, and it was the first time I had ever seen anyone actually shrink. It seemed that his whole body wilted as it might in time-lapse photography, one minute sturdy and stalwart and about to attack, and the next, completely deflated. Suddenly he put his elbows on his knees, bent forward, and hid his face in his open palms.

"Oh, my God!" I heard him whisper.

That seemed to be the moment to hit him again. Still leaning against the door I raised one foot, unbuckled my boot and pulled it off, and then the other one. Then I took my jacket off, unbuttoned my belt, and slid my chinos down. The situation had reversed itself, from my wanting him as an authority symbol during the time we lived in Berkeley, to my being the boss . . . now.

My cock was hard and ready.

"By any chance," I said, "you want to go on bein' a member of the city's finest?" I had two fingers at the base of ole Betsy, gently waving it up and down.

He looked up, his face stricken.

"Since you've already been recorded for the archives," I said wryly, "another one more or less won't make any difference, will it? As I remember, you used to be a fairly good cocksucker, and I got a good load here." And despite my jacking off during the episode with him and Art, I really felt more than ready again. Excitement of the situation, I suppose.

He started to speak, but couldn't until he wet his lips. "Is . . . Is this one being filmed too?" he asked in a dry, husky voice entirely unlike his deep bass.

I shook my head. "Why bother? We've already got enough on you."

I could see the tumult going on inside him—could almost feel it. And then, the more I thought of it, the more I liked the idea of having a handsome pig on call. Usually it was the other way around. Suddenly, I felt burly and dominant again, the ego restored.

"So?" I said, still waving Betsy.

He nodded mutely.

"Okay, man," I said. "Come and get it."

He got to his feet, a little unsteady, and came over to the door. Then, without any further commands, he sank slowly to his knees in front of me. I spread my legs a bit apart and felt the cold doorknob press into my butt again.

He opened his mouth, closed it, opened it again, and grabbed my cock in his big square hand, advancing his head slowly toward it.

Then he shut his eyes tight and inhaled deeply, and took my cock inside his mouth. I drew my breath in sharply and reached down, prying his fingers loose from the shaft, and with my other hand at the back of his head, pulled him closer and closer until I felt his nose flat against my pubic mound. It was all in.

Sheez, it felt good after all those months! I shifted until the weight of my shoulders was against the door, arcing my hips forward a little, and slid both my hands to the sides of his head, holding it steady. Then I began to fuck his face, inch strokes at first, gradually increasing in length and depth until a good four or five inches was traveling in and out of those lips that had scolded motorists, laughed at winos, and

100

harassed homosexuals, down into that deep throat where my cock had always felt completely at home. I shut my eyes and tilted my head back.

I had such a hardon that I thought the skin of my cock could stretch no more, and the head of it tingled as if it had been rubbed with nettles. It was so sensitive that I could even feel the little brush of his uvula, dangling at the back of his throat as it slid softly against the back-and-forth thrusts of my cockhead. But I wanted more than to shoot my wad into his throat. All of a sudden I wanted a kind of symbolic union with Art Kain, and I knew how to get it.

"Okay, Mac," I growled. "I ain't gonna make it too easy for you. Get the hell over to the bed and bend over the edge of it."

He took my cock out of his mouth and looked up. "Ah, hell, Phil," he said, "that Art guy hurt me pretty bad. I'm sore."

I laughed, raised my knee and planted my foot against his chest, and pushed. He went over backward, catching himself on straightened arms just the way I had once caught myself when he pushed me in Berkeley. "Hell, man," I said, "another one's not gonna kill you. We wanta get your asshole stretched back into a useful shape, don't we? Here you've gone all this time without being fucked . . . and now you're gonna get it at least once a week like a good little boy, ain'tcha?"

I could tell he was miserable, but he got up and went to the bed. He looked at me only once, a glance of clean pure hate, and then he bent double over the bed, his legs spread wide apart. I saw the glistening shine of the load Art had left there.

"Guess I ain't gonna need any spit," I said. "Guess it's sloppy seconds for me."

I bent my knees slightly, lining up my cockhead with his asshole, which looked pink and bruised from the battering Art had given it. I dug my thumbs into his cheeks about an inch from his asshole, and pulled him open wider. He yelped.

And then, before the sound of his cry died in the room, I sank my cock into his hole as deep as I could go. The second cry echoed the first. And it was soft and wet inside, clutching at my cock like a sun-warmed melon, seeming to create a vacuum the farther I went in.

And the tingling went on, too. It seemed that the whole of my being was concentrated in that rod of flesh that joined us together, and that this mild electricity was being generated somewhere deep inside his ass or in the tiny girders and hardened tissues of my cock.

At first he was completely passive, until I started straightening my knees on each forward thrust, and rising on my toes, and then sinking back on the outward pulling, for I knew that particular motion, sending my pelvis around in a kind of vertical circle, using his asshole as a fulcrum, was prodding and pushing against his joyspot. He could not remain entirely passive under such treatment. Little by little a few faint sounds escaped him, his head turned sidewise on the sheets. After a coupla minutes of that special handling, I was rewarded by feeling his hips start a small motion of their own, round and round gently, as he invited my cock to the sides of his asshole where it had not gone. And then suddenly he let go with his old familiar cry of "fuckmefuckmefuckme-fuckme!" and grinding his hips wildly, pushed hard with his ass back against my cock on each inward thrust.

I let go of the side of his ass with my right hand and slid it underneath his body, feeling the hot wetness of his sweat alongside his balls. Fumbling in his crotch, I clutched at his rigid heavy-veined cock, standing as stiff and straight and proud as it had during our first encounters. I began to jack him off, rubbing my thumb against the underside of his cockhead, feeling the moist pearls he had put out.

He let out a short clipped yap of joy when I grabbed his cock, and started working his hips back and forth now, setting up a hard backthrust against my inthrust, and cried over and over again "Ohfuckmemanfuckmeman!" his whole body convulsing, using his elbows for leverage to thrust himself back against me. And coolly, calmly, I looked down at my driving cock, watching the sweat shine on his back, and feeling the growing tightness of his tunnel on me.

At that moment I think I had never felt better, more superior, and then in the way of my objectivity there interposed the thing over which I had little control. I felt a tightening in my loins and the muscles of my thighs grew harder. I crouched over him, sealing my belly to his back with our sweat, while his short groans of ecstasy mounted in pitch and number. He ground his cockhead hard into my clutching fingers, and then I felt him begin to come—great shakings of his body, twisting and turning, while each spurt of his gyzym contracted his asshole around my cock and pressured the whole length of it.

He beat me to the peak of the mountain by about two seconds, and then my hand filled with his slippery, thick white come. I let go of his cock and thrust both hands down beside his balls, drawing his ass tightly against mine while time after time I shot into him. My whole body shivered in spasms, tightened in every muscle, and with a great gasp I fell even more against him, pinning him to the bed while all my flesh quivered, and the last of the jets, weakening, spurted into him, to lie and mix with the white flood that Art Kain had left there a half-hour ago. And in the curious postorgasm fluttering of the fantasy that always took place, I felt a double reward: my seed mixed with Art's in a symbolic mating, and my belly and hand smeared with (I almost laughed) who knows how many little Larrys running around in tiny blue uniforms with tinier billy clubs and invisible handcuffs and revolvers.

Beneath me his body was still trembling slightly. I freed my hand—the one still wet with his gyzym—and ruffled his hair with it, thinking that he'd wonder later at the stiff patch that would stop his comb.

When my panting stopped, I raised up with a sudden

103

movement , pulling my cock out quickly without any warning at all. None of the tender recovery stuff with him. He gasped in surprise. The inside of his thighs was wet with the gyzym from the two loads he'd taken.

With my face turned away from him, I felt a slow smile forming. I stepped to the washbowl and picked up a washcloth from the half-dozen ranged neatly beside it. I put some hot water on it and tossed it to him. "Clean up the side of the bed," I said in a hard tone, "where you dribbled down the sheet."

Then I soaped my cock and balls, and washed and dried them on one of the hand-towels on the other side of the bowl. That done, I went to the bed, inspected the cleaning he'd done, and picked up my chinos, drawing them on. He stood in the middle of the room, one hand still clutching the washcloth, looking somewhat like a tourist lost in a foreign country.

"Wash up if you want to," I said, bending to put on my socks and boots.

He did. I glanced at him as he was busy, and felt a contraction in my chest that I hated and loved at the same moment. One of his long handsome legs was stretched to one side as he soaped his cock and balls, and then he cleaned up his ass as best he could. For just a moment I was in Berkeley, watching him at the same task, his long hair hanging down to hide his face. And then I was back, seeing on that same fine mobile face the scowl reappear, his mouth drawn and unhappy. "C-could I use the bathroom?" he asked.

I waved my hand toward the door. "Second on the left," I said. "Then come back here. I wanta talk to you a minute."

"Anybody out there?"

I shook my head, knowing damned well they were all groping each other or giggling behind the one-way mirror. He went out the door naked.

I grinned, made the gesture of success, a circle with thumb and forefinger, towards the mirror, and got up to put on my leather jacket and get a cigarette. I didn't know whether Jerry was still filming, but I supposed he was. He frequently got his most spontaneous and effective scenes by shooting when no one knew it.

Larry was back in about three minutes. He started to dress, glumly, without saying anything. I blew a cloud of smoke in his direction.

"Well," I said. "Something sure backfired. Got anything to say about it?"

He shook his head, still glum. "I blew it, that's all."

"I reckon you did," I said.

"Wh-what's gonna happen?"

"I don't know what Jerry's got in mind for you," I said. "I suppose he'll want to be tipped off in advance in case there's any raid planned on this joint, or know about any other undercover guys the P.D. sends around. And I reckon you'll tell him, because this time, ole buddy, he's got you sealed and delivered."

No word from him. He bent over to dry his calves and thighs, his still swollen cock a-dangle in front, heavy with the remaining blood.

"But why don't you ask me what I've got in mind?" I asked sardonically.

"Well . . . what?" Very surly.

"This," I said. "One night a week from now on, you're either gonna blow me, man, or I'm gonna fuck you. I'll be generous," I said, grinning. "We'll arrange your schedule so you won't have to take a night off when you're supposed to be working . . . and we'll also take my busy nights into account. But come hell or high water, buddy . . ." and here I really grated at him, "you'll show up here or I'll come to your place, or a copy of that film goes right to the Internal Investigation department. And just so you don't get any ideas . . . Jerry'll have one copy at his lawyer's office, and he's havin' one made for me. Soundtrack and all."

Man, I felt diabolic! I let it sink in a moment, and then said, "Okay?"

He did not speak.

"Well?" I demanded.

The slightest of nods.

"Okay, man," I said. I got up from the bed and walked to the door. "You can get dressed now, fuzz, and then Jerry'll tell you what he wants from you. And leave your home phone and address with him . . . that is, unless you'd prefer havin' me call you at the Hall of Justice."

I went out into the corridor, leaving him paler than ever, and closed the door to Tex's room just as Jerry came out of the camera room, grinning like a Cheshire cat.

He rubbed his palms together. "Beautiful, man . . . just beautiful," he whispered. "Couldn't have been a better scene if we'd rehearsed it a month."

I grinned back at him. "You tell him what you want," I said. "And you get his address and phone number, too. I'm gonna relax."

"You think he'll make any trouble?" Jerry asked.

"If he does, just holler," I said. "I'll come a-runnin'. But something tells me he'll be meek and mild."

"Phil," Jerry said, clapping me on the shoulder, "you're the best."

"Oh, sure," I said ironically, and went into my room. I shut the door and flopped on the bed, happy as a whore who's two-timed her pimp.

Blackmail is an ugly word to most people. It suggests white-faced human weasels who call regularly to demand money to keep their secrets. But somewhere along the line I'd seen something about its first meaning—an exchange between the Scottish lords and the robbers of the border, to avoid plunder. But it was an exchange of labor or cattle, not money. And did such an exchange include *pigs* too, as well as cattle?

That wordplay tickled me so much that I laughed out loud. He'd held me in a kind of voluntary human bondage while we lived together in Berkeley. He grew harder and tougher as his police training slowly drained him of his street philosophy, his qualities of love and gentleness and understanding. I watched them be replaced with a new gruffness, an authority that the masochistic part of me worshiped, but the male part of me despised. I'd been his cunt when he needed relief, a kind of physical and economic convenience. And I had watched our relationship slip slowly downhill from a mutual enjoyment and reciprocation to a sort of base servitude where the seed of hate found fertile ground. And then his final treachery in trying to turn me in to the fuzz as a male whore . . .

Love and hate—my God, how close they were together! I'd been his thing, almost a possession, losing my identity in wanting to please him and to satisfy the deep-buried masochism that had so long been a part of me. And now, what a turning of tables, a reversal of the scales, a holding of the whip hand! Mine to play with, to boss around, to fuck. A new delight warmed me as I felt the surge of full authority return. It was not necessarily physical (though that would be a part of it), but primarily psychic, the kind he'd exercised on me . . .

Crossing one boot over the other on the bed, and then recrossing, and actually humming a little, I was completely pleased and satisfied.

I was gonna have the time of my life, man—*in a pig's ass!*

9. The First Instalment

The next day was bright and full of the sunshine that San Francisco produces so well when there's no smog—clear as a dry sauterne, and sometimes seeming to have small sparkling motes of light in it. There was a lot of sky, intensely blue, and some low tumblings of heavy white clouds here and there on the horizon. It was a good day for more camerawork, and that's what we did.

I would never be able to understand Jerry's mind, nor how it could hold together the various segments of his movies in any kind of order, for he never shot chronologically, of course. He always seemed to have a low and squeaky budget, and the whole film never appeared until he set himself to the lonely sweating task of editing, cutting and snipping here and there, agonizing for thirty minutes over which one of two frames he preferred, rearranging in a highly complicated technique called A and B rolls, with black leaders set in A to cover the inserted B footage, and vice versa—and then the equally complicated making of an inter-negative from the original positive, adding a black and white mask, and finally getting an answer print with compensated exposure . . . I was happy enough that the technical aspects did not concern me, and contented to be his "star."

He had spent the rainy days in chasing down and arranging various locations—a bar on Folsom Street, a locker room in a gym, a corner of an underground parking lot—and those were all ready for shooting on the next rainy day. Sunny days were for outside scenes, and so away we went to Lake Merritt in Oakland (which by dialogue magically became Lake Michigan in Chicago), and then to Mount Tamalpais, where there was a dandy outside bucolic scene of my screwing a dude named Charlie—and getting two hundred bucks for the day's work, plus my nuts off in a really wild fragment of an episode involving a bed of nettles.

But there'd been some trouble with the Easter Kid segment. Jerry hadn't been able to find a motorcyclist handsome or intelligent or well-hung enough to take the part—and still willing to be photographed in a blue movie. So between us we sliced that episode away, and tied the other three together with a black-and-white continuity of me getting the hell scraped outa my prick by an amateur cocksucker in the underground parking lot. And considering the state of the country and the emotions between blacks and whites, I also tried to get Jerry to cancel the Ace Hardesty episodes, telling him they'd never go in Philadelphia or New York. But he held firm on those . . .

Tuesday was overcast again, so that day we did the inside scenes—the bar (at nine ayem . . . hell!), the locker room, and the parking lot scene—all of which cost me only one orgasm. Jerry figured that it was better not to ask any of his characters to pop more than once a day, although there were times when he asked me for two or three, and I could usually oblige, provided he got the scene right on the first take. He believed in an extended filming of the actual act, using sometimes all his cameras at various angles and distances so that he could throw the beauty of all the cocks and asses on the screen.

Those two days took care of Monday and Tuesday, and by damn, if it wasn't raining again on Wednesday. I opened one sleepy eye about eleven in the morning, looked at the clock, listened to the rain outside, and in that pleasant half-state between sleeping and waking found myself thinking of life on the farm—cows and chickens and pigs, and pork cutlets and sausages . . . and pigs . . . and pigs . . .

Larry had disappeared, of course, the night his cover was blown, and there'd been no further word from him. I rolled over in bed with a hardon and fumbled in the nightstand drawer for his address and phone number. I swung my legs out of bed, yawned, lit a cigarette, and shook the sleep out of my head. Then I dialed.

"Uh . . ." came a sleepy bass voice on the third ring.

"Larry? Phil Andros."

"Jezuss!" he said. "I . . . jus' got to bed at nine this morning. What in hell you want?" He was very sullen . . . even irritable, in his inflection.

"On night duty, huh? Well, I just wanted to tell you . . . tonight's your night."

"Aw, hell, Phil . . ." he said, coming more awake. I didn't give him a chance.

"Working midnight to eight a.m., huh? Well, that's dandy. I'll expect you here on Mason Street tonight at ten. You'll make it, huh?"

There was a pause, and then he said, with an odd kind of hopelessness in his voice. "I reckon . . . I can."

"Okay, bud," I said, real cheerful. "And Larry . . . you go right from here to the Hall of Justice, huh?"

"Yeah . . . I 'spose."

"Then you'll be in full uniform," I said. "I'll see you at ten. Sharp." And I hung up the phone, very pleased with myself.

About a half-hour more of dozing—and planning—and I finally did manage to get up. I took a shower and shaved, and then moseyed back to the living room for a cup of Jerry's black'n'strong from the ever-hot pot which held about five gallons of coffee.

Jerry looked up when I came in. He'd been working on his

110

double set of books, and was scowling.

"Guess who's coming to dinner," I said grinning.

He looked startled. "I already got a dinner engagement," he said. "Out."

"Nah," I said. "You may want to get back early. Larry Johnson at ten o'clock in full uniform. He's comin' to eat me. I'm the dinner."

Jerry's eyes sparkled. "Goddamn," he said. "More action?"

I nodded. "Thought you might like to get a few shots," I said, "of the stalwart guardian of law'n'order, our blue centurion in uniform suckin' my cock."

"If this goes on," Jerry said, "I'll end up with enough film of him for a full-length feature."

"That'd really blow the SFPD right off the map," I said.

"You can get his badge number tonight," Jerry said.

"I've got an even better idea," I said. "I'll let him take off his uniform coat and then I'll pick it up and try it on, just for the hell of it, and stand directly facing the mirror, close in, and you can photograph it."

"Phil, you're a wonder," Jerry said. "That'll be the clincher."

"I'll tell him to put it back on," I said, "and get down on his knees for a little preliminary skull work. Then how'd it be if he drops his pants and . . ."

". . . and you fuck him right in front of the mirror," Jerry said enthusiastically. "Say, whyncha charge him about twenty-five bucks?"

"Not me," I said. "And you wouldn't say so either if you'd just consider. There you get into different areas . . . extortion plus blackmail plus copulation . . . all felonies. You press him too far and he's just likely to throw the whole thing over, to get even with us . . . with me . . ."

"Yeah, you're right," Jerry said. "Well, why not you give *him* ten bucks? For services above and beyond the call of duty?"

I laughed. "I doubt if he'd take it," I said.

"You could just hand it to him as a part of your insult . . . your 'treatment' of him. Very casual-like. Just tell him it's taxi fare to the station, or to buy a beer or something like that."

"I might be able to get away with it," I said.

". . . if I could just get a shot of your handing the money to him, and then record what you both said . . ."

"Yeah, it's a good idea, all right," I said. "I'll try, but he may not."

"I'll be back by nine to get it all set up," Jerry said.

We let it go at that.

It was a long wet afternoon. I couldn't stand the TV soap operas, and besides there were three dumb studs watching them, so I went back to number seven to read a dirty novel for a while, and then dozed some more. About four o'clock I had a phone call from one of my regular customers, a college prof who lived in Oakland, but I begged off and postponed it until the next day, even though I was losin' forty bucks. But I didn't want to deplete my store of pearls on that particular afternoon; I was anticipating the night too much.

During my dozing that afternoon, I found myself thinking that it would really be exciting to see him again all dressed up . . . to kill. Handcuffs, gun, billy. I'd seen him often enough in full uniform in Berkeley while he was going to the Academy—long-legged, arrow-straight, dark-blue, with the gleaming golden patches on his shoulders, the visor of his cap down almost on the bridge of his nose . . . Hell! there I went again, feeling ole Betsy harden up with the fantasy. I guess I'd have to face it. Despite all he'd done, I still found the bastard attractive and exciting. Maybe even desirable.

Jerry put on his best clothes and left about six. One by one the other models drifted away, until only Teddy and I were left. Teddy made a salad and put a coupla lousy TV dinners in the oven, and we ate in the living room.

"Gonna be some more action tonight, huh?" Teddy asked.

"I guess so," I said.

Teddy threw his long hair back out of his eyes, and drew one foot up under his butt as he sat on the sofa. "And here I thought we might have a repeat while Jerry's out," he said.

I shook my head. "Not tonight, kiddo," I said. "I'm savin' the juice to polish his badge. Besides, I said 'some of these days,' not next week."

"Oh, well," Teddy grinned. "I can always beat my meat while I'm watchin' you fuck your cop, and pretend he's me."

"Sure," I said. "Now you're getting the idea. That's the way to become self-sufficient."

"However," he said, and made a grab for my basket. I got out of his way, and we wrestled for a moment, laughing. The kid was amazingly strong.

He broke away, panting. "Now look what you've done," he said. He had a hardon, and he made it jump in his pants.

"Save it," I laughed. "More enjoyment later. You gotta learn to balance your pleasures. Choose 'em."

"Okay," he said grinning. "But I sure am gonna have you again."

"Other way around," I said, pretending to be tough. "I'm gonna have you."

"Oh, sir!" he said in mock horror, and I swatted him on his butt.

Jerry got back at nine on the dot. This time he and Teddy had to handle everything; Davey was on a call. I went to Tex's room and tucked a ten-dollar bill under the lamp on the nightstand.

Sure enough, promptly at ten the doorbell rang. Being a cop had at least taught him to be punctual. I left Tex's room, thumped lightly on the door of the camera room as I passed, and went to the front door.

My heart almost failed me when I saw him. The rain had stopped, and he had his raincoat over one arm. But he looked so tall and straight, so fuckin' handsome as the hall light hit the brim of his cap and picked out the hollowed planes in his smooth-shaven cheeks, hit and bounced back

113

from the polished badge and the buttons on his jacket . . .

"Come in," I said.

He did, not speaking. He saw a stand in the hall and hung his raincoat on it. Luckily he didn't have that damned white rain-cover on his cap, and I saw with relief that he did not have his walkie-talkie with him.

"Where?" he asked.

I shrugged. "Doesn't matter," I said. "Nobody home to-night. Might as well go in the same room we used before."

His back jaw muscles were working. "I ain't gonna be photographed again, am I?" he grated.

"Hell, no," I said. "Film costs money . . . and we got all we need."

He went in the open door to Tex's room. Jerry had once more jimmied the switch, and I flicked it up and down. "Goddamn house," I growled. "Fallin' apart. This light's been on for days."

He said nothing. He took his jacket off and hung it on the back of a straight chair, then reached for his gun belt.

"Don't bother," I said.

He looked startled. I picked up the jacket and put it on. It fit fine. I walked to the mirror and pretended to admire myself. "Well," I said, "I always wondered what it'd be like to be a cop." I faced the mirror, sure that Jerry was getting a good straight-on view with his camera.

"As if you didn't know," he growled.

"Ah, been doin' your homework, huh?"

"You told me when we lived in Berkeley," he said in a hard tone.

"So I did." I took off the jacket and handed it to him. "Put it back on."

He looked surprised. "Why?"

"I want to know I'm bein' blowed by a real cop," I said. I unbuttoned my chinos and pulled ole Betsy out. Despite all the things working in my mind, she went on happily leading her own life—a hard one. Then I positioned myself in profile

114

to the mirror, spreading my legs apart.

"Blow me," I said, my cock stiff. "On your knees."

He started to take his cap off. "Leave it on," I said.

He lowered himself slowly. "Phil . . ." he began, and then choked.

" 'Member how you used to bully me in Berkeley?"

"You liked it," he said sullenly.

"Ah, well," I said cheerfully, "you'll learn to like it too."

He was on his knees now, and he reached up with a big hand and grabbed my cock at its base. His fingers felt hot and moist. Careful not to let my left arm hide his face from the camera, I put my right hand behind his head, my thumb working down at the back rim of his cap until I'd tilted it far back, so that the camera could get a good square shot at his profile. He opened his mouth and began to suck my cock.

I knew that it was only a performance, that I should have kept my cool, but goddamnit, there are some things you just can't ask flesh to bear. I liked the feel of his mouth on me, and the ten hours of anticipation had brought me to a peak of excitement that I hardly ever felt any more. I took my left hand and loosened his fingers from around the base of my cock, and then—camera be damned! I put both hands around the back of his head, crushing his cap, and started to fuck his face.

He was resting his palms flat open on his thighs, but after about six or seven deep thrusts (gagging him once—the contractions were tight), I felt his hands climb up the back of my thighs, over the chinos, and finally press hard against my working hips, pulling me as deep as I could go into his throat, past the fire-ring, hitting the backwall.

Suddenly he choked, and I paused. "Okay," I said. "That's an appetizer. Now stand up and drop your pants."

"Oh hell," he said. "Not that again."

"In a pig's ass," I said, chuckling faintly.

He did as he was told. I dipped a coupla fingers into the cream and smeared it on his asshole. "Now bend over, ole buddy," I said, "and grab your ankles."

"Keep that fuckin' stuff off my uniform, will yuh?" His voice was muffled.

"Say please."

"Please."

"Okay." I pulled his uniform jacket up and turned it over his back, and pulled down the pale-blue rayon briefs he was wearing. "Why the sissy shorts?" I asked. "You wear them just to please me?"

He didn't answer.

I unbuttoned my chinos and let them slide halfway down my thighs. Then I grabbed his hips and lined my cock up. I touched the head to his asshole and didn't stop. I didn't really ram it into him, but I didn't wait for him to open either. When I punched his sphincter he gave out a stifled yelp and let go of his ankles, but I pushed him back down again.

"Just hold still, pig," I said.

And I started humpin' him—not slow, not fast, just regular. I figgered I might take an hour, leavin' him good and raw and sore for his night's work.

I decided I might as well start out by givin' him my own version of the Art Kain swingaroo. I placed my feet apart to get a balance, and with them as anchor points, I started to swing my hips from side to side in a horizontal line, which—as I warmed to my work—began to peak in the middle when I passed directly by his rosy-brown little asshole. Looking down, I could see it now stretched wide, its lips curling and uncurling with every side movement and inthrust I made. But that rhythm pattern turned out to be too regular, so I varied it, pushing forward first at the left side of my swing and perhaps again in the middle, and maybe withdrawing at the right side. *I should have some East Indian music for this,* I thought.

But there was music forming in my head—a song of a different kind. All of a sudden Larry became a symbol of the persecution we club members had suffered ever since a noble old patriarch named Moses had codified a set of laws to keep his exiled errant flock in line. *Thou shalt not lie down with mankind as with womankind; it is an abomination.* Well, you never make a law unless the popularity of a "crime" compels it. The children of Moses must have been a hot race of menfuckers.

But anyway, it didn't apply to me. I was not lying down with mankind. I was standing up.

I closed my eyes, the better to see not only Supercop grabbing his ankles there in front of me, looking silly with his uniform coat pulled up over his head, his bare ass exposed, and his trousers crumpled in a pile around his calves, but also to see a similar line of young centurions ranged up, stretching to infinity, each one waiting for the vengeance of the Lord to strike him from behind. *My rod and my staff shall comfort thee . . .*

Damn, it felt good! and from the moaning under the coat, it must have affected him too. His tunnel was hot and tight, as I remembered it from a year ago. He started a small motion of his own, straining his knees together on each inthrust of mine, the better to tighten his asshole and clamp me. I knew that he was enjoying it as much as I was.

I zinged along, happy in my work. The fantasy behind my closed eyelids swirled and changed. The long line of bent-over cops merged into others — sailors (their dark blue jumpers still on, trying to keep their white hats on their heads while grabbing their ankles), construction workers with brawny legs and funky crotches, blacks with little tight play-pretend buttocks darkly upended, weight lifters with great smooth marble thighs, and motorcyclists smelling of grease and oil and leather.

I'd planned a good hour's fuck for Larry, but again I hadn't counted on the ten hours of looking forward that I had spent. I hadn't been at it for more than ten minutes when the doors opened and the heavens fell, scattering us both with stardust and leaving about eight good stiff jolts of gyzym in him.

I was so mad I could have killed him—or maybe myself, for popping off too soon. I hung onto his back the way you would a life raft, and losing all detachment and feelings of revenge, reached around for his cock. It was turgid, hot as hell, steaming. I pumped it once, twice, and with a stagger he shot all over his trousers. With my cock still inside his ass I walked him over to the bed, about three steps, his feet tangled in his pants, and mine in mine, and fell on top of him against the bed-edge. We were both panting as if we'd run a coupla miles.

Much as I hated to, I got on with the performance. I pulled out of him quickly, as if I considered him no more than a mere machine for my pleasure, and slapped him on the ass. "Okay, buddy . . . you can clean up if you want to."

"Damnit!" he said violently. "I've got come all over my pants!"

"At least I kept the grease off your jacket," I said slyly.

Awkwardly, shuffling his feet and holding his trousers at mid-thigh with both hands, he made for the washbowl . . . and the mirror above it. That would give Jerry a helluva good shot. Then he soaped his cock and balls with a washcloth and took another clean one, wet with water, to wipe away the spilled gyzym.

"Just look at that," he growled.

"Tain't mine," I said.

"The crease is all gone," he said.

Well, you make up your own lines in *commedia dell'arte*, and that was my cue. I reached for the ten dollars tucked under the lamp. "Sorry," I said. "Use this to get 'em cleaned and pressed."

He looked furiously at the folded bill. "Not on your life," he snapped.

"Aw, c'mon, Larry," I said, grinning my friendliest. "I was responsible for gettin' 'em dirty . . . just have 'em cleaned on

118

me. Or have a beer or a taxi or sumpin'."

He put out his hand reluctantly, but he took the bill. I could almost hear Jerry and Teddy whoopin' behind the mirror.

While he was putting himself back in apple-pie order, fuzz-neat, I washed ole Betsy and tucked her away.

"Phil," he said, "this can't go on."

"How you goin' to stop it?" I asked. "I think it will go on, ole buddy . . . until *I* decide *I've* had all I want. Which may be some time."

"Isn't there anything I can do?" he asked, desperately.

"You're doin' just fine," I said, grinning. I reached up and squeezed his biceps.

He yanked away, angrily. "So help me," he grated, "I'll get you for this if it's the last thing I do!"

I waggled my hand. "You tried that once," I said, calm enough, "and it backfired, remember? And some day you can tell me what kind of deal you pulled to get out of that dope-stash in the house in Berkeley."

He opened the door and stepped out into the hall. I could hear his teeth grinding.

"And listen, Larry," I said softly, "next time *you* call *me*. Next Friday, let's say. I want a lot more of that hot asshole of yours. And," I added, "I sure as hell hope you don't leak out all over the seat of the squad car tonight."

He stormed down the corridor, grabbed his raincoat from the stand, opened the door and slammed it shut behind him, so hard the glass rattled.

Amused and satisfied, I walked down the hall towards the camera room.

10. Wet Boots

We all worked very hard for the next seven days, and Jerry was like a madman, hardly eating, hollering at us sometimes, though he was usually quite soft in his speech. By the end of that time we were all finished with shooting the major episodes and scenes in his film. There remained only some small loose ends for camera-work before the thing was ready for editing and sending to the processor.

Seven days of such activity left me richer by several hundred bucks, but it sure played hell with the activities of the stable. Time after time Davey and I had to cancel, and Jerry even used the faceless Pete and the lanky Tex in a coupla scenes, taking them out of circulation.

Nothing much else happened during that time, except that one evening I came back from a score I'd managed to slip in sidewise, and found a skinny pimply-faced guy of about twenty-one sitting in the living room.

"Hiya," he said, and got to his feet when I came in. He stuck his hand out. "I'm Duke," he said.

"Phil," I said, and shook his thin hand. He wasn't very attractive, and I wondered if Jerry planned to add him to the stable. Jerry was in the kitchen, eating bread and honey — part of his organic food kick.

"Damned stuff's too sticky," he growled, trying to balance the bread so the honey didn't slide off.

"You ought to try eating it the way the ancient Phoenicians used to," I said.

"How's that?"

"They'd put some in a woman's cooze and eat it out," I said, grinning.

"Ugh," Jerry shuddered.

". . . or they'd put some on a cock and then suck it. Creates quite a bond between mouthflesh and cockflesh. To say nothing of the taste."

"At least that sounds more appetizing," Jerry said.

". . . for some people," I said.

Jerry finished the last bite, and turned on the faucet, twiddling his fingers under the water. Then he said, "Duke's kinda down on his luck. Just here from New York and looking for a job. I told him we can't use him as a model since we're full up, but I might find something for him to do."

"So," I said, not very interested. "Say, when's the print due back from the processor?"

Jerry shook his head. "A week, maybe," he said mournfully. "But do you know sumpin? We forgot that scene where the kitchen faucet breaks and we have to send for the repairman. We gotta take that. I've got the repairman sequence all finished, but that damned faucet thing's gotta be done."

"Oughtn't take long," I said.

"We'll do it tomorrow morning," Jerry said, "or maybe tonight. Then I can send it special to the processor and it'll be back in time. Lord knows there'll be enough editing on the other stuff to keep me busy until that faucet scene gets here. Will you help tomorrow?"

"Sure," I said, "but why not right now?"

"We need someone in the laundry room to feed the hose into the faucet and turn the water on cue," he said, "and Teddy went to see his parents tonight."

121

"I kin help," Duke said eagerly.

Jerry washed his fingertips again. "Well, okay, Duke," he said. "It's simple enough. Phil is talkin' on the phone, see . . . and at the same time gettin' ready to wash a plate. So, when he says on the phone: 'Okay, I'll be there tomorrow night' he'll turn the faucet when he says 'night.' And that'll be your cue to turn the faucet back in the laundry room. We feed the hose-end right through that hole in the plaster and point it straight at him. He'll get all squirted with water and have to take off his T-shirt and chinos."

"Is that what I was wearin' in the episode at the time?" I asked.

"What else? I never saw you in any other outfit."

"Okay," I said, "I'll go get ready." I went to number seven and got a pair of chinos and a clean T-shirt, combed my hair and went back. Jerry had the lights set up in the kitchen, the mike boom hanging over the sink, and the camera ready on tripod. The prop phone was on the drainboard, and the plate.

Jerry came out of the laundry room where he'd been instructing Duke. "Okay," he said, and switched on the side lighting.

It was a simple enough scene. I tucked the phone between shoulder and neck, leaned my butt against the drainboard, the plate in one hand. Then I reached over to turn on the faucet and said, "Okay, then I'll see you tomorrow night —" and shit! straight out from the faucet came a blast of the coldest wettest water I'd ever felt, a complete surprise even though I'd known what was ahead. I guess my body wasn't prepared, only my mind. I looked straight up to the ceiling, still holding on to the faucet, and hollered "Goddamn it to hell!" The plate sailed up in the air like a frisbee and crashed in the sink. At that point Duke had sense enough to turn off the water.

Jerry had cut the camera and was bent double laughing. He couldn't stop. "My god," he finally managed to gasp.

"That was the best reaction I ever saw!"

Duke came in timidly. "D-did I do all right?"

"Too goddamned well," I growled, looking down at my cold, soaked front. There was water all over me and the floor.

Jerry recovered, wiping his eyes. "D-damn, that was funny," he said. "Now we just gotta finish your undressing. Grab the faucet again and turn it off. Look at the ceiling and pick up on 'hell.' And then strip off the T-shirt and take off your boots and chinos."

"My boots are fulla water," I grumbled.

"Here," Jerry said, coming with a teacup, "we'll fill 'em up and then you can slowly pour the water out when you take 'em off." He poured half the cup down in one boot, half in the other. I felt as if I were standing in a small Canadian lake.

"Okay, let's roll it," Jerry said. "Duke, stay out of the way."

We got through the rest of it all right. I gave the faucet a vicious twist, hollered 'hell!' and then looked ruefully down at my dripping chinos. I bent down and took off one boot, held it up and slowly poured the water on the floor—and then the other one. I skinned off my sopping T-shirt, undid my belt buckle, and got out of my chinos with difficulty. I turned my ass three-quarters to the camera, because the water-shock had really made ole Betsy shrink, and if you're gonna be a pornie star, you can't let your public see your cock all washed away.

"I'm gonna dry off," I said. "I feel like a water nymph."

Jerry was still laughing. "Okay," he said. "I'll mop up."

I went back to number seven, stuffed my boots full of old newspapers, and put on a dry T-shirt, some clean chinos, and my other boots. Then I went back to the kitchen. Jerry had just finished mopping the floor. He pulled out his wallet and gave Duke a ten.

"Thanks a lot, kid," he said.

"Where's my money?" I growled.

"Aw, c'mon," Jerry laughed. "I'll take you to dinner. Okay?"

"I'll order the thickest steak on the menu," I grumbled.

Jerry grinned. "Okay," he said. Then he turned to Duke. "Can we drop you someplace?"

"Thanks, man," Duke said, folding the ten. "I'll mosey down to the Tenderloin and see mebbe if I kin score."

"All right," Jerry said. "See you later."

Duke went down the corridor and we heard him close the front door.

"Poor guy," Jerry said.

"He ain't much," I said.

"Nope," Jerry said. "He's got one of those long thin ones . . . a virgin's friend. Doesn't rearrange your guts much when he fucks you. Matter of fact, most guys would ask if he was already in."

"Why you bother with him?"

Jerry shrugged. "Ah . . . you know me."

Indeed I did. He was the kind of guy that had a big warm heart and went around collecting little lame yellow dogs — good for a touch almost any time, when he had the money. Take it away, and there was no one more difficult to con out of a five.

"Yeah," I said. "You're an easy mark. A pushover. Ole roundheels."

"Well," Jerry said, a bit defensively. "He just got out of the pokey for car theft, and he's got a long record."

"Not a good one to have around," I said.

"Nope." And then he dismissed the whole thing. "Well . . . you wanta go out for dinner or not?"

"Sure, man."

We got in Jerry's car and headed for the PS on Polk Street — a congenial bar and restaurant, even if it did appeal mostly to the fluff crowd. But who's to complain? Whatever turns you on seemed to be the modern cliché, excusing everything and condemning none.

It was a damned good meal and I was ravenous. The flirtatious waiters and the maitre d' made it all very friendly and relaxed, although I couldn't help wondering what a straight's reaction would be if he wandered in by mistake.

When we got back to the old bordello, it was very quiet. No one was there at all except Jerry and me.

"Wanta watch TV?" he asked.

"Hell, no," I said.

He was sitting in an armchair, drumming his fingers on the leather. "Damn," he said. "I sure miss Teddy."

"How would he know you were gonna be horny tonight?" I grinned.

"More to the point, how do you know?" Jerry asked.

"The signs, man, the signs," I said. "Ole Kinsey used to say that every time you saw a guy tapping his foot or jigglin' it up and down on the rung of a barstool or anywhere else, he was havin' a sexual thought go through his head. And man, you been jigglin' 'em as if you had the palsy or something, all evening long."

"Never heard that before," Jerry said. "Didn't even notice my doin' it."

"Comes from the subconscious," I said. "You wouldn't."

Jerry went on tapping his fingers. Finally he said, "I need a little oral gratification."

". . . and be untrue to Teddy?"

"Aw, c'mon," he said. "I know Teddy plays around some. And so do I."

"Anything in it for me?" I asked, sardonic.

"You're mercenary."

"Just a matter of business."

"Look," Jerry said, and there came the Earnest Look again. "You've made about fourteen, fifteen hundred dollars on this film . . . why not throw in a small sixty-nine?"

"Sex gets monotonous," I said.

"Unless you change partners all the time," he grinned.

"Oh, hell," I said. "Why not? It's a dull evening." My pearl

125

factory was still in good working order, and its daily output was satisfactory, not yet slacking off. Lord knows what my periodicity was—sometimes less than an hour, sometimes three or four, and occasionally a full day. Variable, I guess. If the madame of the house wanted to swallow them, I supposed that I might oblige. And Jerry after all, though not my type (whatever the hell that was), was at least not as much my antitype as some of the scores were.

I unfolded from the sofa. "Your room or mine?"

"Yours," Jerry said, wetting his lips. "Just in case Teddy comes home."

Jerry left one lamp burning in the living room and we went down the quiet hallway to number seven. I turned on the small rosy fucklight by the washbowl, and sat down on the bed to pull off my boots. Wearing less than he did, I was naked first, and stretched out on the bed, hands behind my head. Then I had an idea.

"Hey!" I said. "It's been a long time since I had a really first-class tongue-bath."

Jerry grinned as he stepped out of his pants and finished undressing. He had a soft body, almost feminine. The definition of his muscles had disappeared, flowed together, under the effects of gourmet eating, the large amounts of wine, the lazy living. In that soft light he had the unisex look of a beatific Botticelli cherub—almost chubby, so that you looked for little wings on his shoulders, or a quiver with arrows slung over his back.

"And I'm just the cat to give you one," he said. Well, that was not exactly a cherub's remark.

He climbed on to the bed, his cock, nicely parlor-sized, hard and sticking up against the soft brown hair of his belly and crotch. I unfolded my arms and stretched them down along my sides. Ole Betsy was quiescent, but in that full-heavy stage, lying languid and yet watchful over against my left thigh.

Jerry began on the inside of my left wrist, his warm tongue

lapping, lapping, flattened and wet, and then slowly moved up to the soft inner spot of my elbow, and then with his hand turning my forearm gently, he licked the topside of it as he went back down to my wrist. All along the left side of my body the skin rose in little chill-specks as the pores hardened, and I shivered slightly. Looking down at his moving head, I also saw my cock, in small jerky movements, begin to expand and slowly lift itself until the head no longer rested against my thigh. Then I shut my eyes and let out a deep breath, prepared to enjoy this ministration to its fullest.

As in everything he did, Jerry was a perfectionist. If he had decided to give me a tongue-bath, then that's what it would be—no skimpy hit-or-miss skipping around from one little love-zone to another, but the full and complete treatment. He finished with biceps and triceps and then nuzzled into the warm damp hair of my armpit and up alongside my neck to the ear, the forehead, the eyelids, the cheeks and nose, and flattening his tongue, brushed it back and forth across my closed lips. Then he moved to the other side of my neck, edging his small mobile pleasure-probe into my ear (gently, oh so gently!) and tracing around the rim of it.

And the plateau of my chest—brushing first lightly over the thick mat of hair, and then with more head pressure and flat tongue, until I felt the tongue's heat against my skin. And a concentration around the nipples, swirling around the circles of the areolas, nibbling at each nipple, working downward, downward, through the confusion of the wider strip of hair that ran from chest to crotch, searching and finding the secret whorls of my navel and probing delicately inside, and down, ever down, to the thicker tangle between my legs, his hand closed around my cock at the base (so stiff now and pointed straight upward!) and then nuzzling again beside my balls in the tender dark region between them and my thigh, and licking and lapping, so that one leg quivered wildly.

I was breathing faster and the sweat had jumped out on me.

I was aware that I was turning my head from side to side. But I did not put my hands on him or guide him in any way . . .

The trip down one leg took quite a while, and my senses responded to all of it. My hardon grew stronger as he headed towards the arch of my foot, lapping, lapping, and finally taking the big toe into his mouth and sucking on it, and then the next, and next — on to the little toe, his tongue now weaving in and out of the inner spaces, doing the figure-eight; his tongue flattened, lapping, lapping at the soles of my feet, my heel and ankle and Achilles' tendon. Then he started on the other foot with a little more speed and pressure, doing the same, each toe lovingly caressed, taken into the hot hollow of his mouth, and finally he worked slowly back to the dark region between balls and thigh on the other leg.

"Damn!" I muttered, gasping. The process had already sharpened and quickened my whole body. It tingled and flamed.

He said nothing but I felt one hand under my hipbone, urging me gently. I turned slowly on my belly, and he moved swiftly to the sensitive hollows behind my knees, down to my feet again, and then back up, working first on one thigh and then the other. My cock was pressed hard against the sheet — oddly, not pointed up toward my navel but down toward my feet — and I bore down with my hips, feeling the edge of my cockhead slide against the bed.

He was now at my balls from behind, and I wondered if he were going to rim me. It was hardly my duty to warn him of the dangers — he knew well enough. And if he wanted to, then let him go ahead.

His tongue licked at the far end of the little bridge between balls and asshole, and brushed against my cock, licking the underside of it (now topside as it headed downward), and then lapped against my cockridge. Then more boldly (his thumbs parting the crack of my ass) he advanced, until I felt his tongue brush against my asshole.

My whole body was now quivering almost without cease,

128

and I smelled the sweat of my armpits, which always increased my pleasure. Then I felt his nose press into the crack just above my asshole, and felt his tongue (pointed now, a strong small, wet probe) dig into the tender furrows and folds of puckered flesh, dig and dig, advancing, circling, retreating, flickering, while the movement of my hips grew wilder—round and round—and the pressure I exerted against my down-pointing cock was stronger.

I raised my head, tilting my neck backward, and felt my feet had risen from the sheet as well. And then, wanting him to sink his tongue deeper into my ass, I suddenly gasped and rose to my knees, my legs spread wide, and then fell to my elbows, my back arched upward, the tumult rising in my loins.

"Jezuss!" I gasped. "You're gonna make me come!"

I still don't know how he did it, but quick as a flash he slid his feet and legs between mine, humped once on the bed, and was underneath me, his mouth beneath my down-pointing cock. And there, flourishing where nothing had grown before, directly below my mouth, was his cock heading towards me. I opened my mouth and took it all inside, and felt him seize my own cock into the burning hollow of his mouth.

"Damn!" I yelled even with my mouth full, as the flood-gates opened and I poured a string of pearls, spurt after spurt of my come, down deep into his throat, and, at the same time, up from his cock gushed his own fountain—powerful jets, but not many. My knees slipped, and I felt the whole convulsing throbbing length of my cock slide down his throat, made even more slippery with my gyzym. And I sank my head down, air rushing in and out of my nostrils, my mouth softly nibbling and nuzzling at his rapidly softening cock. My own was so deep in his throat that I was choking him; with his hands he pushed upward against my groin to signal his need for air.

With a groan I rolled off him to the side, forearm across my eyes, my chest heaving with the storm that had shaken me.

But he twisted his body sidewise after taking one gasp of air, and sank his mouth on my cock again—softer, gentler—forcing its head to rotate in his mouth, using the pressure and movement of his tongue, ever more gently, until finally he raised his head slowly, still faintly nibbling at the end, getting that last small pearl to add to the string.

"Damn, boy," I said, reaching down to knuckle his head and tousle his hair. "It's a cryin'... shame you keep that... talent all to yourself. You oughta be a workin' stable-stud yourself. You're good!"

"That's high praise ... from you," he said, grinning a little. "I don't do all that much ... for anyone I don't like."

"I envy Teddy," I said.

Jerry shook his head sadly. "I can't do that for him," he said. "He's too damn ticklish."

"Pity," I said, and lay still. My blood pressure was almost back to normal.

Just then the phone rang back in the living room. "You answer," I said. Jerry pushed the proper button and picked up the phone, answering with the number.

I heard the receiver vibrate. "Yes," Jerry said. "Just a minute." He handed the phone to me, silently mouthing "Your cop."

"Yeah," I said.

"Phil? This's Larry. It's Friday. You told me to call."

"Yeah, man," I said, straightening on the bed. Jerry had one hand still on my cock, pulling gently at it. "How's your schedule this week?"

"I'm off Sunday night at seven," he said gruffly.

"How's about I come to your place around eight?" I asked, winking at Jerry.

"... Okay ..." Hesitantly, grudgingly.

"Fine," I said, bright and cheerful. "I'll see you then."

I hung up and laughed. "Well," I said, "ain't life beautiful?"

Jerry chuckled and laid his cheek on my cock. His tongue flicked softly at one ball. "Whatever turns you on," he said.

130

11. Up Your Ear

The next afternoon I was lying on my bed in number seven, fully dressed, reading a book with one hand and gently caressing the bulge of ole Betsy with the other. I was nearly asleep. The door was half-open, always a sign in the old whorehouse that you didn't mind being disturbed if anyone wanted to talk or visit. Several persons passed by from time to time, but no one stopped.

No one, that is, except Jim, the dude whom Jerry used as a cameraman, the one who'd given me the first-class toejob on the way back from San Gregorio beach. He knocked tentatively, and at my "C'mon in!" he pushed open the door and entered.

"Hi," he said. "Whatcha readin'?"

It was an old dogeared copy of Euclid's theorems, which I'd used for years as a sleeping pill. I showed him, and told him what it was.

"For chrissake," he said disgustedly. "A fuckin' snob."

"Not me, man," I grinned at him. "I'm Greek, remember? This calms the mind."

" 'Euclid alone hath looked on beauty bare,' " he quoted.

"Now who's a fuckin' snob?" I demanded. I threw the book on the bed. "What're you doin' around the joint? The movie's finished."

131

"I know," he said, sitting on the edge of the bed. "Just came over to see if I could pick up a little free sex." He grinned widely with his generous toe-grabbin' mouth.

"See the manager," I said gruffly.

"He ain't here," Jim said. I looked at his well-shaped earnest butch face, and the flattop of his black hair, wondering idly if the short hair indicated he was a real nonconformist, or just a play-pretend one.

"In that case," I said, yawning and stretching, "it's up to me. I reckon I really couldn't charge you for your specialty, account I like a toejob as well as the next one."

Jim looked down, a little shy. "I got another one too," he said.

"What?"

"FFA," he said.

"Oh," I said wryly. "Future Farmers of America."

He shook his head. "No," he said, "it means Fist—"

"As if I didn't know," I cut in. "Whatdyuh think I am . . . an amateur?"

"I might have known you were on to it," he said.

"Damn," I said, "you are a real specialist, ain't you? That must mean you've done everything else. Real jaded . . . at twenty-five, is it?"

"Twenty-six."

I'd gone through the fist routine only about a half-dozen times with my scores. There was a big chapter of the group in San Francisco. It was dangerous unless you knew what to do, and a helluva lot of bother considering all the preparations. And it was a curious thing about the fisters; they were the ultimate "in" group, or so they considered themselves, even more than the S/M bunch. Once you'd had the experience, nothing else ever seemed to satisfy. It was a little like communism; it took away your sense of humor. They were deadly serious about their specialty—had their party towels and beach bags with emblems, even matchbook covers monogrammed with two interlocked stylized figures, shoulder patches, posters, keyrings, and T-shirts, all with the fisting symbol.

Jim picked up my right hand and looked at it. "I don't know if I could take that," he said. "That's an engineer's hand. Big and square."

I grinned. "Others have managed," I said. "You gotta know how to do it."

He looked at me with clear grey eyes. "How about it? I can afford ten, plus a toejob and blowjob, if you'll just do it. We could go over to my pad, so that if Jerry came in he wouldn't know."

"Where do you live?"

"I'm stayin' with a guy over on Pearl Street. He's at work."

"Pearl Street?" I said.

"Pearl was one of the early madams. And you know all those alleys and streets named Minna and Jessie and Clara and Clementina? They're all named for old San Francisco madams of whorehouses. He was very nervous.

Funny thing about my reaction to his proposition. I'd done the fisting so seldom that I was really interested to try it again.

"Hell," I said. "Let's do it just for fun. Forget the money." The real truth was I liked anybody who liked me, like most hustlers I guess, and I was flattered that a husky, handsome stud like Jim wanted to have a second round with me.

Jim sparkled, and gave off with another wide grin. "Let's go," he said.

He had a little Volkswagen out front and we buzzed over to Pearl Street. "The playroom's in the basement," he said when we got there.

It looked like a horror chamber, musty, dismal, with a naked light bulb dangling like a hanged felon from the ceiling. One wall was completely filled with whips—little cockwhips, twisted willow ones, bullwhips, razorstrops, and (Jim said) an oxwhip from Red China, a Danish one with a crocheted handle, and an Egyptian one with mosaic insets and a camel-stabber concealed in the handle. The wall at an angle to the whips had a big collection of handcuffs, leg-irons, chains and assorted gimcrackery, even prisoner-boots of iron.

"Who-o!" I said with a low whistle.

"Carl's into the S/M scene," Jim said, "as I reckon you can guess."

The basement was warm from a furnace tucked away on one side. There was a doctor's table on the other side, with raised steel supports and curved braces angled out at one end, the kind used to examine a woman's widespread cooze. Jim had modified the supports by adding straps that evidently buckled over the knees, once you were flat on your back with your legs spread wide and elevated on the steel uprights. He'd also added some buckling straps to hold the arms at the sides.

"While I'm cleaning up," Jim said, pointing to a washbowl on the fourth wall, "you can do your surgical scrub. The nail file and clipper are on the ledge."

He grinned and disappeared into a walled-off john.

Meanwhile, I went to work. First I undressed and then put my boots back on (the floor was cold). I clipped the nails of my right hand down short and then I filed them smooth and cleaned out the residue beneath. After that I took the square blue cake of 2% Neko and lathered my hands and right arm up to the elbow, rinsed, and did it again. I didn't wipe them on anything, but held my arms bent up at the elbows, like a doctor waiting for his gloves. They dried in a little while.

Jim came naked out of the john. He whistled. "Man, oh man!" he said. "I'd forgotten how big your dick was."

"The better to fuck you with," I said, and then seeing his dismayed look, added, ". . . later."

He had a well-made solid body, about five-nine or ten. I remembered it from the time he blew me in front of the mirror back in the old whorehouse. And he sported a good-sized cock, about half-hard.

"I remember seeing a dirty movie," he said, dreamily. "A hustler was fist-fuckin' a guy, and after he got his hand in, he stuck his cock in too and jacked himself off inside."

"First things first, buddyboy," I said. "Up on the table."

He climbed up and got in position, flat on his back, legs high. He winced a little at the cold leather as he lay down. "Cold," he said, fitting his underknees over the curved steel supports.

"You'll be warm enough in a little while," I growled. "Where's the Crisco?"

He pointed to a low table on which sat the familiar blue-and-white can. "You'll have to help me buckle in," he said.

"But I've scrubbed."

He turned his head up and back. "See that roll?"

I did. It looked like a roll of paper towels. They were polyethylene gloves "printed" on tissue paper. I tore two off and stuck my hands in them. Then I buckled the straps around his kneecaps.

"My arms too?" he asked. His mouth was so dry that he could hardly speak and he had a raging hardon. So did I, for that matter.

I fastened the sidestraps around his shoulders, under his armpits, and his wrists to the sides of the table. He was immobilized. Then I grabbed his calves and scooted him down on the table until his wide-stretched asshole was just a little below the bottom edge.

I stripped off the gloves, scooped up a handful of Crisco, and smeared it over my right hand and forearm, wiping my left hand on the tissue paper which had held the gloves. I stepped over between his legs.

"I suppose I don't need to tell you to relax," I said.

He shook his head negatively on the table. "No, man," he said, his voice scarcely recognizable because of its choking huskiness.

Well, I thought, *here goes*. I drew my fingertips together into a kind of cone and pointed them directly at heaven's gate. When I first touched his asshole he jumped.

"Easy, man," I said, and then realizing how deep an M he was, I added, "You'll either take it clear up to the elbow, or I'll leave you strapped and go out and get a few buddies and let them have a go at you. And," I grated, "I'll pick the ones with the biggest hands and you'll wish you never left the farm in Indiana."

The fingers started to go in and got as far as the first knuckles, when they were stopped by the strong ring of his sphincter. I used my left hand to swat him hard on his upstanding cock, knocking it to the right. It was almost purple by now with the engorged blood.

"Relax, damnit," I growled, and he did. After a moment, the sphincter gave way and I went in to the second knuckle. I looked at his face. His eyes were closed and he had an expression compounded of both ecstasy and pain; his forehead was wet with sweat. And gradually his hardon was disappearing. With a series of small pushes I got all five fingers in, rotating them slowly back and forth, and boring with pressure. And then I twiddled them a little against the hot encircling flesh. He gasped and moaned, turning his head from side to side on the table.

"Shaddup," I said, very basso. Getting the whole hand and knuckles in was something else. The sphincter resisted mightily. Coldly, almost clinically, I kept up the one-third rotation, at the same time forcing my hand forward. He began to make small animal sounds of pain.

"Shaddup, I told you!" I said, slapping his cock. "You asked for it. Now you're gonna take it . . . all." I gave a fierce push with my arm.

Heavily greased and succumbing to the force of my thrust, the sphincter was unable to resist any longer. It opened suddenly, and my hand passed through. He let out a great cry and his torso arched upward. "Ah-h-h . . . oh-h-jee-zus!" he shouted.

I was inside. It was like plunging your hand into hot, cling-

136

ing wax not yet entirely melted, all-enfolding, pressing tightly against my skin and at the same time resilient, a kind of hot-glove sensation. I moved my fingers slightly, tentatively, and he gasped. Then I slowly began exploring, stroking first one sidewall and then the other, knuckling the top and bottom softly. His ass began to move, up and down and sidewise, and his face was now heavy with sweat that began to roll off the sides of his forehead.

"Oh, fuck!" he moaned.

And just what was that small kernel locked behind its thin wall of membrane? I touched it, and with my index finger pushed gently against the side of it, and then grasped it with three fingers — oh, so delicately! — and squeezed a little, a small, blind, velvet caress. I thought his scream of pleasure, not of pain, would bring the neighbors running. It was the mysterious dark prostate, with the vague shape of the vesicles just beside it. I lightly fingered it all around, dancing my fingertips over it, feeling its attachment and the cord running from it, rewarded by the quivering and arching of his whole body. A few thin drops of milky fluid seeped from the end of his cock and glistened as they ran down the shaft.

"Can . . . you get . . . your cock in beside . . . your hand?" he gasped.

Well, nuthin' like the old school try. But he interrupted again. "P-popper," he said. "Down . . . on ledge. At foot. Underneath."

I couldn't see it but I moved my left hand along the bottom of the table and found it. Then, by feel, I stuck the blunt end of it towards his buckled-down hand. He took hold of it and I unscrewed the bottom, smelling the sharp, dirty-foot smell of butyl nitrite as it spilled into the room. I pressed forward between his legs as far as I could. It took a lot of fingerwork, but I inserted the open end in his nostril, closed the other with my thumb, and he took a deep breath. I withdrew it quickly, took a deep one myself, and put it in his right hand, screwing it shut.

137

The popper hit him about ten seconds before it did me. In the meantime, I stuck my cock up along the inside of my right wrist and slipped it in. He groaned again but I paid no attention. My cock moved slowly in beside my wrist until I felt the crown of it in my palm, and then I began slowly to jack myself off with my fingertips. The popper was making him writhe, and when it hit me I was not sure I could stand up. With my hand and wrist still inside I masturbated myself faster, gradually lowering my body until my right ear was resting on his belly. The nitrite flickered a hundred fantasies through my head, lightning fast, dissolving, withdrawing, speckled with green and blue and red lights. In less than thirty seconds I popped inside him, while his gyzym spurted just below my chin. He was gasping like a fish removed from water, and my own panting was heavy, blowing through his pubic hair.

We were both exhausted. I kept my hand inside, moving it slow as old time, caressing the sides gently, easily. He managed to stretch his fingertips and put them against my hair, sighing. And then I began slowly to withdraw both cock and hand. He arched his body again as the knuckles came out, and then his body melted, its tensions gone. He sighed again, deep from his gut.

"I feel . . . as if I'd just . . . given birth . . . to a baby," he said.

I laughed. "You did, ole cock," I said. "This baby—" and I raised my gleaming hand and made a fist. "Small enough to be premature, but . . ."

"But large enough," he said. He exhaled deeply. "You ever been bottom man?"

"In this kind of deal?" I asked. "Not me, buddy. I'd sure have to trust the guy that tried it. 'Spose you got somebody who'd rip your carburetor out. Besides, I don't think anything that big would go in."

"Ah, hell," Jim said. "If you wanta try it sometime, you can sure trust me."

"Not today, Mac," I said, wiping off the grease on a towel he'd laid out. "Maybe sometime when I'm hotter than I can stand." I put the towel aside. "I'll unbuckle you before I scrub again."

"Okay," he said, and I did. He vanished into the john and I lathered my hands and forearm. Well, if it was his bag . . . okay. But I wasn't sure it was mine.

I dressed while he was in the bathroom, and when he came out he was dressed too. I looked at his firm shapely ass, so tightly clutched by his Levi's that the crack showed, and thought of the wonders of that dark, hot, red cavern, the sensation of the wildly pulsing contractions when he shot his load (so different from the same contractions around a cock!), and the mysteries of the location of the parts, with my hand like a blind explorer learning them by touch, there in the most secret places of his handsome body. I shook my head a little; I didn't want to get hung up on this parasex, this sex so far beyond the limits of what's called both normal and abnormal. Of course, I'd had my cock in there, too, but I wondered if the California penal code had anything in it forbidding a hand-in-the-ass instead of a dick, and decided it didn't—the legislators hadn't even thought of that one yet! And if some congressman dared bring it up on the floor of the assembly, the shock and disbelief of his colleagues would insure that at least a decade would pass before they were able to face the problem and legislate against it.

But it was a real sensation, all right! I looked again at his midsection, so firmly enclosed in denim, the bulge so noticeable at the front, and again could hardly believe that there had been room inside for my hand. I remembered how my fingertips had danced and scampered over the sacred stone, traced the tubes and muscles, and how my knuckles stroked the arching tunnel and felt the second sphincter, closed to me. What lay behind that Bluebeard's door, and could you get through that one without triggering every alarm in the castle? Well, time enough to discover, to explore farther.

Jim took hold of my biceps. "Damn fine, man," he said. "Do it again, sometime?"

And me, ole cocksman that I was, nodded and said, surprisingly enough, "Yeah, and maybe the next time I will be bottom man, just for the hell of it."

He squeezed my arm even tighter, and grinned. "Kinda got to you, did it?"

"Yeah," I said gruffly. "Gonna run me back to Mason Street?"

"Sure thing," he said, and we got into the beetle and drove through the streets, tortured, and narrow and one-way, until he headed down the hill from California Street, and stopped in front of the whorehouse door. Once in Helena, Montana, I'd seen a sign on Wood Street in the red-light district, the only neon ever advertising a brothel. It read *Ida's . . . Rooms With Girls*, not *for* girls. I wondered when San Francisco would be ready for that.

The house seemed curiously quiet when I let myself in. "Anybody here?" I hollered and there came a muffled voice from the back bedroom . . . Teddy's. "I'm . . . back here," he said. He appeared at the doorway, holding a film can. Even from that distance I could tell that something was wrong.

"Hey . . . what gives?" I asked, closing the door quickly and walking rapidly down the hall. As I got closer I could see that his eyes were red, and the hand that held the film can was trembling.

"Oh . . . my god," he said, his voice breaking.

"What the hell's the matter?"

He brushed at his eyes with the back of one hand. "Look," he said.

The room was in chaos—drawers opened, contents spilled, filing cabinet forced open (the lock broken), a mess in general. "Shit!" I said. "What gives?"

"They . . . got Jerry," Teddy said unevenly. "Search warrant. They went through all the rooms, even yours, but they didn't take anything except the film. The last one before

140

. . . not the new one. And they . . . arrested him."

"What the hell charges?"

"Something like 'aiding and abetting . . . oral and anal copulation,' " Teddy said. "They took all the pictures 'n' everything. And they also got him for running a 'disorderly house.' "

"How'd they get any evidence?"

"Aw," Teddy said, "you remember that sonofabitch that was here while I was visitin' my parents? The one that helped you shoot the faucet scene?"

"Duke . . ." I said.

"Yeah. Well, he was a fink . . . a police informer. Seems he swore that after he turned the water on, he stayed and watched Jerry film a scene between two guys screwin' each other, with Jerry tellin' 'em what to do."

"Nuts!" I said violently. "There wasn't anybody here except Jerry and me. And we all know Jerry never allows an audience for the sex scenes. Duke was no more here than on Mars."

"But he said he was," Teddy said.

"He wasn't. Where's Jerry now?"

"At the lawyer's. He's already out on bond of ten grand."

"They didn't get the new film?"

Teddy shook his head. "How could they? It's not back from the processor yet. I tol' you . . . it was the one before last. And only the original . . . not the answer-print."

"Well, that's safe then," I said.

"Jerry told me to call the L.A. man," Teddy said. "I did. He was scared."

"Jerry can beat the rap," I said confidently.

Teddy shook his head. "But I think Marv won't fight. He's withdrawing. Says he's got too much to lose."

A thought came to me. "Could that fuckin' cop have had anything to do with it?" I demanded.

Teddy shook a negative at me. "Don't think so. No mention of him as complainant."

Well, I could understand that. We had too much on Larry Johnson. I'd be sure of his guilt or noninvolvement after Sunday night . . . tomorrow. But I imagined, knowing a little about the inner workings of police departments, that all too often the left hand doesn't know what the right is doing. And after Larry blew his assignment and was put back on patrol duty, well, he'd be entirely out of touch with what went on in the vice and narco divisions. And for damn sure, with all the film on Larry (still at the processor's, and lucky for him that it was!), he'd never even have tried to swing a warrant!

"Lucky," Teddy said. "All the other guys were out when the fuzz came. And now they've all moved out. It looked like the exodus from Egypt." He grinned, and a little of his old buoyancy returned.

"Why didn't they arrest you? You're a minor."

He grinned again. "I was back in the crawl space behind the washing machine," he said. "An' when I heard 'em, I just stayed there. Are you gonna move out too?"

"I don't see why," I said. "They've got nothin' on me. I'm just a roomer, and I'd like to see 'em prove different."

"Oooh . . . they might," Teddy said. "They took all the pictures of the stableboys in the hallway, and wasn't yours there too?"

"No, it wasn't," I said. "There's no chance of their provin' anything." But even as I said it, I felt a cold wind blow over me. Perhaps, just perhaps, this was more the time for discretion than bravado.

Suddenly Teddy's bounciness was gone and he was just a frightened kid once more. "Ph-Phil," he said. "I'm sc-scared shitless."

"C'mon, man," I said, and put an arm around his shoulders, feeling fatherly. "Worse comes to worst, you can get a motel room until this blows over. Maybe stay with me somewhere. Anyway, I'll bet a dollar Jerry'll be home tonight."

But all at once, feeling his head turn and his face bury itself in my leather jacket, I felt the anger rise in me and my back teeth bite hard together.

"There, kiddo," I said. "Don't worry." But ole Betsy— damned individualist that she was—began to straighten and unbend in a most unfatherly manner, as I felt his young body press against me, trembling.

12. Love and Death

They say the wheels of justice turn exceedingly slow — but sometimes they go like a whirlwind. Jerry had come back the night before from a long consultation with his attorney, looking pale and drawn. His smut-angel in Los Angeles had developed more than cold feet; he was turning state's evidence, and as reward would be permitted to leave California without prosecution. Jerry's arraignment was set for Monday morning.

"No possibility of a delay or continuance?" I asked him, Sunday noon.

Knees drawn up under an old bathrobe, Jerry shook his head. "Not with Marv's deposition," he said. "All I can hope for is suspended sentence and probation." His fingers nervously intertwined, then disengaged only to tangle again. "I guess this little gold mine is closed down."

"But all the world's makin' dirty movies," I protested.

Jerry swallowed noisily. "My lawyer thinks it's not that they want so much to get me for the films as for keeping a whorehouse."

"What about this last film? When are you gonna edit it?"

Jerry twisted his knees and sat on his feet. "If I get probation, I'll do it next week," he said. "But not in the City. I'll go over to Alameda County and hide away at a friend's house up in the Oakland hills." Then he looked at me. "What're you gonna do?"

I shook my head. "Find myself a place to stay," I said. "Something tells me this joint is gonna be padlocked sooner or later."

Jerry nodded. "Sooner, probably," he said. "I'm going to get dressed now and drive to Sunnyvale to pick up the processed film. And I'll get our copies of that film of your cop."

"Both segments?" I asked. "Not only with Art Kain but with me?"

"Four hundred feet altogether," Jerry said. "One part with Kain . . . the second one with you."

"It's Sunday," I said. "Aren't they closed?"

"I called Friday, even before the bust. Yeah, they're closed, but they left the film at the front desk with the security guard."

"Has it been paid for?"

Jerry sighed. "At least that's one good thing. They got Marv's certified check Friday for the whole fuckin' schmear. No sweat there." He untangled himself from the sofa and stood up, managing a thin smile. "Well, I might as well get dressed and start for Sunnyvale," he said.

I punched him on the shoulder. "Okay, man," I said. "Good luck. I'll be here when you get back, I think. Maybe I'll even chance stayin' the night and leave early tomorrow."

"All right," Jerry said. "But I wouldn't stay any longer than that if I were you."

I went back to number seven, took off my boots and socks, skinned off my pants and jacket, and then stretched out naked on the bed, pulling a thin blanket about halfway up.

What a Goddamned country we lived in! I think that perhaps it was the blatant hypocrisy that got me most—a real disaster stemming from our heritage of puritanism. Our

145

legislators made laws that conformed to the Judeo-Christian ethos, and could hardly wait until their daily sessions were over to break them. Totally lacking a sense of history, they went on and on, holding themselves to the Old Testament in theory, but enjoying the wildest life of the senses in practice. Puritanism, optimism, and hypocrisy — the three-footed pedestal on which the stars and stripes would float forever, by God!

There'd always been prostitution and always would be. I wondered what the lawmaking dummkopfs would have to say if any of them realized that their beloved Thomas Aquinas had once said that prostitution was necessary to social morality, just as a cesspool was necessary to a palace, if the whole palace were not to smell. Or that St. Augustine had said that without prostitution the sanctity of the family could not be maintained. As long as a man had a stiff cock and a desire to bury it in some warm and cozy nook, he'd find a whore to help him, whether male or female. But still the shallow boobs, the lawmakers, went on, trying to control the deepest and most potent urge of man (aside from self-preservation) by piddling little rules telling him the proper conditions under which he was permitted to get a hardon. As if a law on paper could control the flame of fantasy opening in the brain at the sight of a good body, or keep the mind from sending its secret messages to the groin, flooding the cock with a rush of blood, and turning the key to the vesicles to let the hot gush spurt out!

Having expelled some of the venom in my head by these pleasant thoughts, I fell asleep . . .

. . . to be awakened in about twenty minutes by a hand on my cock. I did not open my eyes, and pretended to be asleep flat on my back. But man alive, there is nothing that rouses one any more quickly or thoroughly than a touch on the dick. Through the narrowest slit of eyelid I saw that Teddy was sitting on the edge of the bed, glancing half-fearfully at my face and then returning his eyes to my cock. I lay perfectly still for a moment, and then stretched my legs a little farther apart so that my balls hung down. At the same time, I bent one arm and shifted my shoulders a trifle—an ordinary sleep movement. *Well, well,* I thought, *with Jerry gone to Sunnyvale, here was the little chicken flapping its wings again.*

His grasp on my cock was not tight, and when I moved he stopped everything to see if I were awake. But I went right on playin' possum, wondering just how many times in the past the same thing had happened to me while I kept up the pretense of sleeping.

Through the unfocused screen of my eyelashes I watched the intentness on his face, the tongue moving outside the lips to moisten them. His hand on my cock tightened gently and then relaxed. And ole Betsy responded, of course, growing by imperceptible degrees in girth and length, the head rising gradually above the thumb of his encircling fist until it was about three-quarters grown.

In the one encounter between Teddy and me I realized that he hadn't sucked my cock at all. I'd just fucked him. All of a sudden I was curious to see what kind of a cocksucker he was—a swallower, a scraper, a nibbler, or whether he could do the vacuum bit, or had to keep his hand at the base because he couldn't take it all.

I made another slight body movement, and he stopped his handiwork again.

His tongue was continually moistening his lips and I heard him swallow noisily. *Get down on it,* I thought, *or I may just flop over and ram it down your throat!*

By now my cock was fully hard, the head of it red and gorged with blood, the veins—from the pressure of his handgrip at the base—standing out along what I could see of it. *You fuckin' little cockteaser,* I thought, *chances are that you know I'm awake and want a blowjob!* I didn't know whether to abandon all pretending, put my hands at the back of his head and force him down on it, or just to relax and let things happen. I decided I'd relax.

I didn't have long to wait. He opened his mouth wide and with one sudden movement took my cock inside, down to his hand, and then, slipping his fingers aside, he went on and on, until I felt his perky little nose flattening against the skin of my belly just above my cock. The whole movement was done so quickly that it was all I could do to keep from reacting. All mouths are different, somehow, and all techniques, and the novelty of a new mouth, even after thousands, always sent me sliding away through a rosy fog.

Teddy's method was nice, a kind of combination of pressure and looseness, with the tongue drawn clear to the back as a sort of hot smooth moist barrier to keep my cockhead from the backwall of his throat. And yet, glancing toward his slowly bobbing head, I saw that his lips on the downward plunge were lost in my pubic hair, and I felt them tightening, then loosening at the base. Where did he put it all, if his tongue blocked the back of his throat?

Since Teddy as a person didn't turn me on too much because of his youth, I set my mind loose to pick up whatever fantasy it could, and draw it into bed with me. With eyes tight shut, I was somewhat surprised that I saw the massive back and shoulders of my ole buddy Art Kain hard at work on my cock, his longish brown hair falling over his face, his huge hard-bunched thighs pushing my own wider apart (it was only Teddy, who'd climbed between my legs so that he could take my cock straight on), and then—Art again—cupping my tightly drawn-up balls in his huge hot fingers, working them with his thumbs while his fingertips made gentle scratching movements in my pubic hair.

He choked slightly and then withdrew to the cockhead, nibbling it gently and sucking it, while his tongue ran small arpeggios up and down the sides of it, curling under the flange of the corona, hardening itself and wedging sidewise into the wet slit on my cockhead, tasting the pearls that had formed there, and with his tongue first on one side and then

148

the other, forcing my cock against his mouth walls, between the warm unyielding surfaces of his teeth.

Suddenly I was in a paint-locker on a Navy destroyer, the hatch dogged and heavy-bolted, and the small Filipino sailor Domingo was hard after my nuts and cock, with the paint-smell heavy in my nostrils. Another shift, or a melting, and there were dozens of naked feet parading alongside me (was I lying on my belly looking flat along the floor?) — the feet of young and naked cops in the shower room at their academy, merging into one who stood scowling over me, a face all too familiar — Larry's, ole Supercop, he with the oversize prick and narrow ass. With his foot he flipped me over on my back and fell on top of me, his hard cock poking and prodding, but never quite getting into my cunt for some reason, and yet myself feeling as if it had, sliding down the slick walls of my vagina, rubbing the clitoris . . .

Ah, goddamn! No female crap . . . ! With almost a roar I opened my eyes, seized Teddy's head between both hands, and using one knee turned him over on his back so that his face was directly beneath my crotch, my cock in his mouth, and not supporting myself on either elbows or knees, growling savagely, my belly tight pressed against his sweating slippery forehead, I started to fuck his throat relentlessly, pressing him hard down on the mattress. The barrier of his tongue jumped out of the way and positioned itself underneath my cockshaft. Without stopping, I plunged almost desperately clear to the bottom, trying with violence to erase that small slit through which the female in me had flickered. His hands were on the front of my hipbones, trying to push me up and off so that he could breathe. He choked, and the constrictions deep in his throat were as fierce as those of the most professional cocksucker.

And still I kept on, pinning him tightly beneath me, while in the middle of my spine the flashes began, the flames caught fire in my loins and one, two, three more — with that the float of red stars falling from zenith to nadir behind my

149

eyelids, a roaring in my ears, and a collapse on top of him while my gyzym spurted down into his throat, choking him, bubbling up around my cock which I kept as far in as I could. And then, with one mighty convulsive heave of his body and push of his arms, he lifted me off him, and my cock, still dribbling its white flow, trailed down his chin and came to rest underneath his jaw.

With his face turned sidewise he took in great gulps of air, unable to talk. I still lay heavy on his head, and then I turned a little to one side. With my hand I reached down to his chin, wet with my gyzym, and laughing, smeared it all over his face and forehead. He still could not talk.

"Maybe that'll be a lesson, buster," I said. "Don't ever attack a sleeper . . . you never can tell what'll happen."

He moved his eyes to look up at me, his head still pinned beneath my body. His face was shining with the undried gyzym. "Good God," he said. "I thought a damn earthquake hit me."

"Gotta remember . . . sometimes people wake up in peculiar ways," I said.

Beneath his thin pullover his chest gradually stopped heaving. "You ain't kiddin' me," he said. "You were awake a long time before you landed on me."

"Yeah," I said. "But why spoil a good blowjob? And lissen, kiddo . . . it was good."

Some of his flippancy returned. "Aw," he said, "you say that only to the scores who pay you."

"And to talented amateurs," I said, mussing his hair a little. "You not only gave me a good job, but you also got an astringent facial." And then—being the last gentleman, as one john once called me—I said, "You didn't come?"

"The hell I didn't," he said, looking ruefully at his slacks. They were light grey, and a large dark spot was down one side of his crotch. "Looky that."

"Tsk," I said. "What'll Jerry think?"

"What he don't know won't hurt him," Teddy said. "I

gotta go change before he gets back. Thanks," he said, "Uncle Phil."

I threw the pillow at him as he closed the door. And then I really did go to sleep, a coupla hours maybe, while visions of sugarplums danced in my head. I was finally awakened by the slamming of the front door.

"Anybody home?" Jerry yelled, and I heard Teddy holler from the back bedroom.

"Yeah, I'm here," I called out at the same time.

Jerry opened the door. He had two small packages in one hand, and under his arm was a large flat carton. "Hey!" he said. "Here's the film I promised you," and threw the two small ones on the bed.

"Thanks," I said. "You got the original okay?"

He grinned and patted the big box. "Sure did," he said. "Now all I gotta do is edit it . . ."

". . . and appear in court tomorrow morning and hope for probation."

"Yeah," he said. Then he grinned, like the old Jerry. "I don't mean to sound inhospitable," he said, "but when are you leaving?"

"This evening," I said. "I'm gonna pack and leave my suitcase in a locker and go pay a final call on my treacherous fuzz."

"Be careful," Jerry warned.

"Don't worry," I said. Then I picked up the two small boxes. "Are these marked? I mean, which is the Kain one and which the one of him and me?"

"You'll have to check," he said. "Come get the cotton gloves so's you won't fingerprint 'em."

I swung out of bed, draped a towel around my middle, and went barefoot back to the bedroom. Jerry handed me the gloves, and just as he did an idea hit me. I said nothing, but went back to my room to think it over.

I'd picked Larry out of the gutter once in Berkeley, up on Telegraph Avenue, and he'd moved in with me until he could get his head straight . . . so what, now, was preventin' me from moving in with him for a time? After all, here is a poor homeless whore, kicked out of his bordello and off his sound stage where things had been goin' just dandy, and wasn't it the motto of several police departments: "To protect and to serve"? I certainly needed protection and service . . . or servicing. And if the city fuzz would by any chance be lookin' for me as an inmate of a disorderly house, would they ever check the apartment of one of their Very Own? The irony of it tickled me. Not that I'd want to stay with him for any length of time, just long enough to jolt him considerably, and show him who was really boss.

I was finished with my packing by six o'clock—just one case for a light traveler, a shuttlecock. Plenty of time to get something to eat and be at Larry's place on 20th Street by eight o'clock. I said goodbye to Jerry and Teddy and wished them well, called a taxi, and took my case to the bus station on Seventh Street and checked it. I kept two things out, the small can of film with Larry and Art Kain on it in the inside pocket of my jacket, and four five-foot lengths of clothesline, which I fitted into a small cardboard box and stuck under my arm, because I had a little plan. When I got to the cafeteria, I wondered just why I had taken the film along; it was my copy, and I needed it to make Larry knuckle under, but suppose he got it away from me somehow? Well, there was the even more damning one of him and me together, with his badge photographed and himself accepting ten bucks, and that was safe in the suitcase in the bus station.

When I'd finished the lousy meal, I went out. It was only six forty-five and one of those incredibly clear San Francisco evenings, with the sky just beginning to lose its brilliance of blue and take on the rose and yellow tints, and throw the long shadows that came a few hours before sunset.

I felt wonderful, and decided I'd walk the distance to 20th Street, about fifteen blocks. Even the ugly Americans looked beautiful this evening, for one reason or another. I was in no hurry going up Market Street, and when I got close to the Castro area where there were many little artsy-craftsy shops, I went into a corner mom'n'pop grocery store, looked around, and bought a very small can of Crisco . . .

. . . for my little plan might really bring a cop down a few notches. And who could tell? Done properly, it might turn him into a Future Farmer of America, and then let's see him find a brother-fuzz who'd perform that small service for him. Get him hooked on it, and then leave him.

I was really puffing by the time I'd climbed the forty-five-degree hill at the hump of 20th Street. The number he'd given me was on an old wooden house with the usual San Francisco bay windows, full of gingerbread wooden carving and Victorian gewgaws and moldings. To insult me further, there were about forty steps leading up from the street.

The front door was a leaded glass one, and a hallway light was burning inside. I pushed the bell under *Lawrence F. Johnson* and waited.

No answer. I pushed again, longer, hearing the bell ring deep in the apartment. Taking a shower, perhaps. I lounged against the doorjamb, looked at my watch and saw it was five to eight, shifted my stance a coupla times, and pushed again.

Then I noticed that the door was not latched, only closed, about a half-inch of molding showing. I put my hand on the doorknob and turned. It was open. I pushed the door back and went inside.

"Larry!" I hollered. Still no answer. I heard a clock ticking somewhere.

I called again, with no response. Hell, it was just like the movies! The door was left unlocked and you always found a corpse inside.

I walked down the corridor. To the left was a living room. Through an arch you could see another room—the bedroom, perhaps. I stepped into the living room.

The hair prickled on my neck. I dropped the box of clothesline. Larry was lying on the bed, naked, one knee drawn up but lying flat, one arm hanging down a little over the edge of the bed. The bedclothes were tangled. From his mouth had come a thin stream of vomit, staining the sheet, and blood from his nose and mouth had long since dried — brown on the white.

"Larry . . . Christ almighty!" I croaked, my mouth suddenly dry and filled with wool. Under the blow of shock you hardly remember what you do, and the mind fills with a thousand things. I think I picked up his arm, feeling for a pulse that I knew was not there, for the skin of his forearm was cold and without life. His cock lay shrunken against one thigh.

And then I saw on the beige carpet a capsule, bright red, and on the stand beside the bed a bottle, empty, prescription label on it . . . Seconal, and his name beside the doctor's. And another bottle, half-empty, of whiskey.

My body was reacting, out of control. The sweat rolled down my forehead, sprang from my crotch and trickled into my chinos. And then my hands started to tremble. I filled my lungs with a deep breath and shook my head to clear it.

The next thing I remember was sitting in an armchair in the front room, shaking all over. He must have been dead two or three hours. Unconscious, he had vomited from the reds which he had taken on top of the whiskey — a fatal combination. And then he had drawn the fluid into his lungs; the choking and coughing had broken a blood vessel somewhere.

Suicide . . . I blinked, and more sweat rolled from my eyelids into my eyes. Suicide . . . that usually meant a note. I looked around the room. There it was, propped against the face of the alarm clock by his bed. Still shaking, I went back into the bedroom, not touching anything, and bent down to read:

Can't hack it anymore. Nobody's fault
but my own. Too many past mistakes . . .

It was selfish, I know, but the flood of relief almost stunned me. "Nobody's fault but my own." For my conscience had already — before seeing the note — tried and condemned me and sentenced me to execution.

They say a dying man's life flashes before his eyes. But now, it was Larry's life that flashed before mine — the things he'd told me and that I'd found out on my own: his involvement with heavy drugs, his smothering of his own child, his childhood as the youngest of identical triplets, his juvenile record of petty theft and car-stealing, the broken home and the uncaring slattern of a mother who'd been a whore.

Larry! Poor damned dead Larry! No more the joys of sex, no more any of the good sensations of life — the taste of pizza with a coke, the feel of warm lips against your own, the tight sliding pressure of an asshole against your cock, or the little teeth-nibblings as someone gave you a blowjob. He could not see anymore the low rumblings of white clouds on the horizon, nor the blue sky, nor the red circle of the sun sinking below the Golden Gate bridge. No more drunken evenings (and only those who have been drunk together can love or understand each other), no more the high of grass which he so loved.

Ah, Larry! . . . And then I looked a little closer and saw the dried semen on the sheet near his crotch. *Well,* I thought, *at least he went out with one final orgasm, and I hope to hell he enjoyed it!* There was a small pearly track leading from his crotch down the inside of one thigh.

No necrophiliac, I — but something drew me closer. I leaned over his body, and reached down and touched his cock gently. And that was enough. The shock of the coldness startled and frightened me, for I suppose that unconsciously I had been thinking that it might still be warm. I drew back quickly, and stood thinking. And remembering . . .

But all that was for later. After a moment of uncertainty, I reached for the note, folded it, and put it in my pocket. I could at least save him the stigma of suicide . . . or make it doubtful. A lot of people overdosed.

I had to get the hell out. Still trembling, I picked up the box of ropes and the paper bag with the Crisco in it and went out through the living room into the hallway. I fished a handkerchief from my pocket, swiped it down the edge of the doorjamb and the inside doorknob, and then cleaned off the outside one, closing the door as I had found it, not quite latched.

The air was cold against my sweating body. But I turned, controlling myself, breathed deeply and went down the steps, stumbling on the last one. I walked slowly and casually down the steep hill, my eye on the phone booth at the foot of it, one hand clutching the can of film in my pocket.

I went into the booth, took a dime out of my pocket, and holding the receiver in my handkerchief, dialed the operator. When she answered, I said:

"Give me the police. There's been an overdose."

13. Epilogue

An Olympic-sized swimming pool, brimful with crystalline and sparkling blue water, a high stone wall with iron pikes, a two-hundred-thousand-dollar house on several levels with a sunken living room — it's hard to imagine such a setup in a burg called Indiana, Pennsylvania, but that's where the big bohunk lived, spending his overlarge salary as a vice president in electronics on all of the creature comforts he'd been denied in the days when he got his muscles working in the coal mines of West Virginia. In California you might have expected such a layout; in the Midwest — no.

The sun was hot. It dazzled the eyes and broke into a million mirrors on the water surface. And it fell sensually on my body and on that of the giant in the chair beside me.

"How much longer can you stay?" he asked, a slow smile lazily curling his heavy lips, parting on his white teeth. One big square hand indolently cupped the bulge of his brief black nylon trunks.

I waggled my hand at him. "How much longer can you afford me?"

"For a long time," he said, grinning. "But I know you. I can see the signs. You're gettin' restless."

"A little," I admitted, arching my body in the recliner and stretching my arms.

"It's been a swell three weeks," he said. "Good vacation for me. But I gotta get back to work come Monday." He turned halfway in the chair. "I really never knew how much fun sex could be."

"Glad you didn't say 'love,' " I said wryly.

And there had been plenty of it on the warm nights, swappin' cans, blowin' each other. We'd done everything in the book and then some, both of us caught and held in the net of sensation—pure sensation, pure sexual activity, the spiraling helix of orgasm after orgasm.

"If you leave, where will you go?" he asked.

My eye fell on the water-spattered postcard from Hawaii that lay beside my chair. "Come on over," it read. "This is a real paradise. Have a look around and be the star in my next film." It was signed: Jerry.

"I don't know," I said. "I honestly don't. Maybe Chicago. But California's spoiled me, weather-wise. I couldn't go back to fighting the summers and winters in Chicago."

There'll be no entrapment of the heart, I thought. I'd never realized how close I'd come until I looked into that bedroom on 20th Street in San Francisco. And even after that, it had taken weeks to understand that the hate I felt for him and what he'd done had spread like ink on a blotter, overrunning the line between hate and love, spreading, diffusing, until the two areas were joined. And why I'd kept that note I'll never know. Folded in my wallet, it had magnetized my thinking, polarized my mind, until even in the wildest gymnastics with Art I found myself thinking of it.

"Excuse me," I said. "Gotta take a leak."

I went into the cool house, but not to the can. I took the steps two at a time to the bedroom he'd given me and got my wallet from my trousers. I extracted the note, unfolded it, and snapped a table lighter into flame. Then I watched the paper turn brown, curl, and the fire spring upward to my fingers. I dropped the note into a large ashtray and looked at it steadily until the ash crinkled and the smoke died. Then I crushed the fragile black sheet with my fingers, and wiped them on my trunks.

I rummaged in my suitcase and pulled out a small cardboard box marked with a penciled "K." I tossed it in my hand, and looked down at its twin, unmarked. I wasn't sure when I'd be up to lookin' at that one—but then, I hadn't seen the one marked "K" either.

I went downstairs, out into the hot brilliant sunlight, and sank into the recliner beside Art's.

"Here's a souvenir," I said, handing him the box. "Be sure you're with friends when you watch it."

"What is it?" he asked.

"A short dirty movie," I said, and then yawned. "If you're goin' back to work Monday," I said, "I guess I'll hit the road again myself."

Other books of interest from
ALYSON PUBLICATIONS

☐ **B-BOY BLUES,** by James Earl Hardy. A seriously sexy, fiercely funny black-on-black love story. A walk on the wild side turns into more than Mitchell Crawford ever expected. An Alyson best-seller you shouldn't miss.

☐ **BECOMING VISIBLE,** edited by Kevin Jennings. The *Lambda Book Report* states that *"Becoming Visible* is a groundbreaking text and a fascinating read. This book will challenge teens and teachers who think contemporary sex and gender roles are 'natural' and help break down the walls of isolation surrounding lesbian, gay, and bisexual youth."

☐ **CODY,** by Keith Hale. Trottingham Taylor, "Trotsky" to his friends, is new to Little Rock. Washington Damon Cody has lived there all his life. Yet when they meet, there's a familiarity, a sense that they've known each other before. Their friendship grows and develops a rare intensity, although one is gay and the other is straight.

☐ **THE GAY FIRESIDE COMPANION,** by Leigh W. Rutledge. "Rutledge, 'The Gay Trivia Queen,' has compiled a myriad gay facts in an easy-to-read volume. This book offers up the offbeat, trivial, and fascinating from the history and life of gays in America." —Buzz Bryan in *Lambda Book Report*

☐ **MY BIGGEST O,** edited by Jack Hart. What was the best sex you ever had? Jack Hart asked that question of hundreds of gay men, and got some fascinating answers. Here are summaries of the most intriguing of them. Together, they provide an engaging picture of the sexual tastes of gay men.

☐ **MY FIRST TIME,** edited by Jack Hart. Hart has compiled a fascinating collection of true stories by men across the country, describing their first same-sex encounters. *My First Time* is an intriguing look at just how gay men begin the process of exploring their sexuality.

☐ **THE PRESIDENT'S SON,** by Krandall Kraus. "President Marshall's son is gay. The president, who is beginning a tough battle for reelection, knows it but can't handle it. *The President's Son* is a delicious, oh-so-thinly-veiled tale of a political empire gone insane. A great read." —Marvin Shaw in *The Advocate*

☐ **TWO TEENAGERS IN 20: WRITINGS BY GAY AND LESBIAN YOUTH,** edited by Ann Heron. "Designed to inform and support teenagers dealing on their own with minority sexual identification. The thoughtful, readable accounts focus on feelings about being homosexual, reactions of friends and families, and first encounters with other gay people." —*School Library Journal*

These books and other Alyson titles are available at your local bookstore.
If you can't find a book listed above or would like more information,
please call us directly at 1-800-5-ALYSON.